KEEPING PAIGE

DIVINITY WARRIORS

MICHELLE M. PILLOW

MICHELLE M. PILLOW® - MICHELLEPILLOW.COM

Keeping Paige (Divinity Warriors) © Copyright 2009 - 2018, Michelle M. Pillow

Third Print Edition July 2018

Second Print Edition September 2017

First Print Edition July 2012

Second Electronic Printing March 2012

First Electronic Printing July 2009

ISBN-13: 978-1-62501-190-9

Published by The Raven Books LLC

ABOUT KEEPING PAIGE

DIVINITY WARRIORS BOOK THREE

Alternate Reality Romance

An outcast because of her psychic abilities, Paige doesn't expect her people to rescue her when a zealous sect of Faerians sacrifices her to their gods. Thrown through a fairy ring to a new dimensional plane, drugged on ambrosia, she is compelled to claim the first man she meets. Only when the effects wear off and she's left with a husband expecting more than she's willing to give, does Paige discover the true extent of what the fairies have done.

Ordered by the king to marry, Sir Aidan of Fall-enrock is dead set against taking a bartered bride. He believes his people should be patient and wait for the gods to bless them. When the beautiful Lady Paige comes through the sacred rings, kissing and touching him like she knows their joined fate, Aidan's sure he's being rewarded—until his new bride tries to back out of their marriage.

ABOUT DIVINITY WARRIORS SERIES

In a land forever at war, the Starian men are so busy fighting that their marriage ceremony has been reduced to a "will of the gods" event where they simply pick a woman out of a lineup and claim her as a wife. With women becoming scarce, it's necessary to trade the offworld Divinity Corporation for brides.

They live a very Medieval-like existence. Instead of medical advancement and technology, all of their focus has been on developing weaponry and battle strategy. With places named for war, such as Spearhead and Battlewar, these men have been left in charge way too long. They are in desperate need of a woman's touch.

DIVINITY SERIES

Divinity Warriors

Lilith Enraptured
Fighting Lady Jayne
Keeping Paige
Taking Karre

Divinity Healers

Ariella's Keeper
Seducing Cecilia
Linnea's Arrangement

MICHELLE'S BESTSELLING SERIES

QURILIXEN WORLD NOVELS

Dragon Lords Series

Barbarian Prince

Perfect Prince

Dark Prince

Warrior Prince

His Highness The Duke

The Stubborn Lord

The Reluctant Lord

The Impatient Lord

The Dragon's Queen

Lords of the Var® Series

The Savage King

The Playful Prince
The Bound Prince
The Rogue Prince
The Pirate Prince

Captured by a Dragon-Shifter Series
Determined Prince
Rebellious Prince
Stranded with the Cajun
Hunted by the Dragon
Mischievous Prince
Headstrong Prince

Space Lords Series
His Frost Maiden
His Fire Maiden
His Metal Maiden
His Earth Maiden
His Woodland Maiden

Qurilixen Lords Series

Dragon Prince

Marked Prince

More Coming Soon!

To learn more about the Qurilixen World series of
books and to stay up to date on the latest book list
visit www.MichellePillow.com

AUTHOR UPDATES

To stay informed about when a new book in the
series installments is released, sign up for updates:

michellepillow.com/author-updates

PROLOGUE

"Oh, blessed fairies of the great forest, givers of spring, and givers of life after the cold! Take our autumn offering to grant us safe winter and bring life after the snow. Take our offered sister and make her a queen of your realm."

"Let me go, you crazed heretics!" Paige screamed, kicking and jerking her limbs to be free of the hands that held her high over a sea of ivy-crowned heads. Outrage pumped hard and fast through her veins until she felt as if her heart might burst from her chest in little pieces. "You don't want me. I'm not a believer. I will curse you with dead trees and wilted flowers. My father's people will not stand for this!"

All right, so the last part was a lie. Her father's people wouldn't care what the Faerians did to her. In fact, she half expected they traded her to the crazed women to be rid of the last of her cursed family. How else would the heretics have known where her hunting ground was located? Or that she'd be there following the buck migration?

The Faerians ignored her pleas and threats, answering the priestess's words with random exclamations of, "Oh, blessed fairies!" and "Take our Forestter sister. Grant us life!"

Long, drifting branches passed over her, the yellowed leaves falling with each push of the breeze. They hit her chest and hips, and fluttered onto the female heads surrounding her only to tangle in their flowing locks. A tiny giggle mingled amongst the swaying treetops and Paige stiffened in horror. Soon the first laugh was followed by more mischievous sounds, as if a choir of fairies watched the procession. She couldn't see them, but that didn't mean they weren't there and very real.

Paige didn't need to see the ground or the pathway in which they traveled to know what was happening. They took her to the sacred circle, to the fairy ring of the great forest to be sacrificed. The trees gave way to a grassy clearing. A ring of stone pillars created a large circle, each roughly carved and three times as tall as the women. Their towering height imposed as it impressed. The believers carried Paige between two of the pillars.

"At least give me back the clothes you stole from me. Don't send me like this!" she screamed, shaking now that they were drawing to the end of the journey. Everyone knew about the fairy rings, had been warned as children to avoid stepping within the fairy playground. Paige's own grandmother claimed to have come through them when she was a young girl. "At least give me my bow. Have some compassion. Don't send me to the fairy world unarmed."

Paige believed in the possibility of fairies, though she had never seen one for herself. From what she had been told as a child, they were mischievous, somewhat vengeful creatures and they liked nothing more than to play tricks on non-worshippers.

"Oh, blessed fairies, here is our sister!" the priestess called. The woman ordered her lowered and Paige felt the cold chill of a stone altar at her naked back. The flimsy gauze they'd wrapped around her waist like a belt hardly counted as clothing. As the material snagged on the rock, the pin holding it close to her hips dug into her flesh.

Paige struggled to be free. A ring of mushrooms

grew in the center of the stones, so innocuous in appearance that if a person didn't know about their hidden magic they might be tempted to step inside. Was this truly the fairy ring, supposed doorway to fairy realm? The truth was Paige didn't know where the ring would lead. No one did. She doubted even the Faerian priestess knew all the fairy secrets. Her grandmother came through and it wasn't the fairy world she had been living in.

The priestess stood over her as countless hands pinned Paige down. The woman's white gown formed tight to her bodice only to flow in long waves along her waist and hips. The skirt trailed behind her in a long train. Tiny gold flowers were embroidered along the hem. Her followers wore the same outfit, minus the embroidery and train. Long, straight black hair seemed to stir around the priestess's oval face, the thin strands dancing like snakes. The woman lifted a wooden cup she had carried with her from the village.

"Drink of the ambrosia," the priestess urged, her gorgeous brown eyes round and filled with promise. "Taste the nectar of the fairy goddess and feel the pleasures of old magic. Let it take you. Let it show you."

Paige clenched her mouth tight, struggling

violently as fingers pressed into her cheeks to force her teeth apart. The priestess's expression didn't change as she leaned over and slowly poured the cup's contents into her prisoner's mouth. Wherever the liquid touched, tingling erupted, almost burning in its intensity.

Paige tried to resist, spitting the liquid out over her face, but it was too much. She was forced to choke down several gulps or drown. The tingling spread down her throat into her stomach and over her cheeks from where trails of discarded liquid touched her flesh. She tried to resist the alluring magic, but it was as useless as resisting the falling rain.

The instant the cup was empty the Faerian women let go, leaving her free to run. Paige shot up on the altar, ready to bolt into the woods to hide, only to be brought short by a transparent winged creature flying in front of her face. Paige jerked back in fright, sliding her ass on the rough stone. The fairy's gown matched that of the priestess, with the train trailing down past her feet as she fluttered about in the air. The creature's eyes looked too big for her face and her skin glimmered, tinged with pale blues and silvers. Silver threads wove in delicate patterns over her wings. Soon more small beings began to appear to her, each tinted with different shades of nature.

Paige couldn't move. The strange sensation of the ambrosia traveled through her blood, leaving her stomach to conquer her limbs. Even her fingernails and hair seemed to prickle. With each passing second, the fairies became clearer. They flew around the gathered worshipers, perching on their shoulders and heads, completely unseen by those who did not drink. Several pulled at the priestess's hair, combing the locks with their fingers to create the snakelike effect she had noticed earlier.

They buzzed around her and Paige jerked, trying to follow them with her eyes. But, when she looked too quickly, the forest blurred into streaks of impossible colors. The Faerians became excited at Paige's apparent visions.

"What madness is this," Paige whispered, swatting at the pests. The flat of her hand managed to smack one across the body and send it flying. Instantly, the others became enraged and attacked. Though Paige tried to fight them off, they swarmed her, pinching her flesh, pulling the long locks of her red hair and the gauze of her belt, pushing wherever they could touch—along the soles of her feet, her exposed sex, her nose and breasts. Paige grunted, flailing about in an effort to be free. With surprising strength, the fairies slid her ass over the coarse surface of stone toward the center ring. For a moment they held her suspended in the air before tossing her at the ground into the ring of mushrooms.

Paige screamed for salvation, but the only answer she received was the high-pitched screech of fairy laughter and the incessant droning of, "Oh, blessed fairies! Take our sister, grant us life!"

1

HANGING FOREST, OUTSIDE FALLENROCK VILLAGE, PARALLEL UNIVERSE

S<small>IR</small> A<small>IDAN</small> of Fallenrock grinned at his good friend Peeter's cherub-faced daughter. When Ileen had blinked her big brown eyes at him and begged him to let her decorate his long blond hair, he had known he would give in to her. The four-year-old had known it as well, for Sir Aidan could never deny one of her requests.

That is why he now found his hair pulled into a messy array of knotted braids and tied with yellow and pink ribbons. He was even sure she had stuck a few flowers and leaves in there for good measure. At her look of pride in her creation, he didn't have the heart to take it down until he was well away from the cottage. Even then, he would need a comb and about three hours of hard tugging.

"Pretty Dandan." Ileen had the look of her mother, dark skinned and eyes with tightly curled hair that bounced as much as she did. Only her nose took after Peeter.

"Beautiful Leenie," he answered, kissing the top of her head before moving to untie his horse's reins from a low tree branch.

"You should wear those ribbons to the breeding ceremony," Peeter teased, doing a horrific job of hiding his amusement. "How could any bride resist you? You'll be sure to fulfill the oracle's prophecy."

Aidan frowned, glanced at Ileen and bit his tongue. What he felt like saying to his friend was not fit for young female ears. Peeter laughed heartily.

"The town oracles have been wrong before. They don't know everything. There's no proof I must take a bride, let alone a bartered one. Besides, the old crones only said they strongly encouraged a marriage." Aidan wasn't sure who he was trying to convince more. The truth was, the oracles had been fairly certain of the signs, but he hadn't told anyone that part of the prediction.

"They have been right, too." Peeter grinned at his pregnant wife. She sat near the front door to their modest home, rubbing her swollen belly. "They said Shana would bear two daughters."

Women were scarce in Staria. With their endless wars, boys had become a necessity and their natural evolution answered the call with more sons than daughters—when they did have children. Their low birthrate wasn't from lack of trying when the warriors were home, but war took them away all too often. Sometimes forever. The fact that Shana gave birth first to a daughter was a miracle and a blessing.

"With enough tries, any man can give two daughters," Aidan teased, hoping to turn the conversation away. King Wilhelm already ordered him to Battlewar Castle in a little over a fortnight to attend the next breeding ceremony. It seemed all of Staria plotted to see him wed.

"So you have decided? You're not going to choose a bride?" Peeter's pity was almost too much to bear. His friend didn't want him to end up alone. "Won't you at least look at the women the king has bartered for?"

"Yea. I've been ordered to do as much." Aidan grimaced. "What if these otherworlders are misshapen or strange in the head? Or worse, cowards? I do not trust this Divinity Corporation to choose women who are right for Starian men. You've heard the tales of how the Divinity man-aliens looked—weak and simpering and endlessly talking.

They depend on their technologies more than duty and responsibility and the power of a full day's work. They do not earn a trip through the fairy rings with the gods' blessings, they build contraptions to force their way where they do not belong. The gods would never bless such overstepping people. Here in Staria we know what is important—duty in battle, meeting your responsibilities as a warrior, as a husband, and as a man."

Peeter suppressed his laughter. "You do not speak of anything I do not know. Are you trying to remind yourself?"

"It is easy for you to be smug. The fairies brought you Shana long ago. If only I had seen her first, then perhaps it would be me laughing at you."

"Ach, she would not have you," Peeter dismissed, his amusement only growing in strength. "Besides, I am much better looking. She would have found her way to me either way."

"Pretty Dandan!" Ileen pouted, pushing her bottom lip out in defense of Aidan as she looked at her father.

"Only because you made him so," Peeter answered. The child giggled and began skipping around the yard in a random pattern.

Aidan scratched at his knotted hair, watching the

child briefly before stating the biggest affront, "Not a single one of those otherworlders carried a sword when they appeared in the midst of battle. What fool doesn't take a sword to a fight?"

"Perhaps the women will be grateful to be away from such weak men. They'll be enamored of our warriors and very willing to—" Peeter stopped talking, giving a conscious glance to his playful child.

Aidan sighed. Every belief he carried since childhood told him it was wrong to barter for otherworld brides, especially when the cost wasn't too high. Nothing good came without some sacrifice. The gods of war taught them that much. Besides, what woman agreed to travel to an unknown world just for a little blue mineral water? The stuff ran in springs beneath the earth. It would be like bartering for dirt or handfuls of grass. "The king should not have meddled in the will of the gods. If they wished for me to find a bride, they would have sent one through the fairy rings as is tradition. Since they have not, I can only assume I have yet to earn one."

"You? Not earn one? You have fought more battles than anyone in the village. The fact the king wishes you to be amongst the firsts to choose from the new blood means you are honored." Peeter firmly gripped Aidan's arm. "The king only wishes to ensure happiness for his people. Is it so wrong for men to want softer company? I don't want you to end up alone, not after all the loss you have suffered."

"Peeter," Shana scolded, not standing from her seat. "Leave Aidan be. His heart will choose what it must. Whether these brides are gifts from the gods or an abomination of Starian beliefs, it is for each man to decide for himself. You have your bride. Leave Aidan to choose his wife in his own way."

"Yea, my lady." Peeter instantly gave in to his wife's command. "As you so desire."

"Thank you, most wise Shana," Aidan said, bowing his head toward her.

"Though, you'd do well to find someone who can cook," Shana said, laughing, "or who doesn't mind that you make bread as hard as rocks."

"Ugh, won't let me forget it, will you?" Aidan swung onto the back of his horse, naturally adjusting into the saddle. He barely had to give the animal directions as it turned from the small cottage on the outer edge of Fallenrock Village. "How do you know I didn't cook like that on purpose, so you would take pity on me while my mother is at sea?"

"That is perhaps the saddest thing you have ever said to me." Shana suppressed a smile. "Very well.

Come back as often as you must, good sir, and you will be fed."

"Now we will never be rid of him," Peeter protested good-naturedly. "He will be at our door like a stray wolf begging for scraps."

"Too late, my friend. you cannot rescind the offer now." Aidan grinned. He said his final farewells before riding into the solitude of the forest. The hairstyle had to be the most unmanly look for a serious soldier of Starian's army and he couldn't ride through town during the daylight hours lest it be seen. It didn't matter if he whiled away the hours in the forest. No one waited for him at home. The pang of loneliness settled once more in his chest, only having been temporarily lifted by the company of his friends.

"Despite what the oracles say, I will stay strong and wait for the gods to bless me. I will not take a bartered bride from another world who I have not earned. When it is time, the fairies will bring her to me." Aidan drew little comfort from the sound of his own voice. Convictions were good and well, but they did not fill his arms or his home. And until after the breeding ceremony, the king commanded him home to get his house in order. Without the thrill of the battlefront, he had nothing to fill his hours but the aching loneliness of his heart and the empty rooms of his home. Regardless, he had made his decision to honor tradition and, once made, a true Starian did not change his mind.

SPRING. It was spring.

Paige stared at the treetops, entranced by the way the sun shone through the limbs to backlight the leaves to a lighter shade of glowing green. Almost dazed, she breathed deeply, taking in the smell of moss and dirt, of bark and fresh air. The warmer hint of a breeze caressed her skin, even though she stood in the shade of the forest. It looked like the great forest, but it couldn't be. It was spring and the great forest was in the throes of fall.

"The fairy realm," she whispered, blinking but unable to see any flying pests.

The fairies must always live in spring. Those crazy Faerians were right. The fairies keep the spring season and only let it loose once a year in my home world. The priestess did it. She sent me to the land of the fairies.

The ambrosia tingled through her senses, making it impossible to feel much of anything beyond the euphoric spell that grew deeper with each passing moment. Perhaps it was a blessing, otherwise she would be screaming in fright at what had been done. Her flesh itched and she rubbed her hands over her arms to make it stop. Unfortunately, touching only made the sensations worse until her heart hammered in her chest and the not-so-curious sensation of desire flooded her thighs. Even the simple act of breathing seemed to incite a wild, uncontrollable lust.

Her nipples hardened, yearning like never before. Paige knew desire, but she rarely acted on it and never had she felt it to this strong of a degree. This must be what the people of her village referred to as the madness of passion. She had never understood how simple lust could make people witless and imprudent or how they could use it as an excuse for their idiotic actions.

When she couldn't run her hands over her chest, shoulders and neck fast enough, her flesh went from itching to burning. The colors of nature became brighter, more vibrant, as if kissed by a light that did not exist. Leaves crunched under her feet, untouched forest litter that tickled her senses and caused her to stare at the ground in wonderment as she half danced, half marched in a noisy circle.

A green spider caught her attention and she

pressed her face close to its back and wondered at the odd shade of its man-size web. Paige lifted her hand and reached to pet the insect's back. "Good day, small creature. So lovely to see you."

"Halt! When they are that shade of green it means they are filled with poison."

Paige blinked as the loud voice boomed over her forest playground. She pulled her hand away from the web, despite the fact she still wanted to touch the spider's fascinating back. How could something so wondrous and beautiful be filled with poison?

"Who are you? Come out from there. What are you doing in this part of the forest?"

Paige leaned around the spider's tree, touching the opposite side to peek at the person who spoke. Her hand caressed the rough bark, gripping it as she pressed her weight forward. She worked her fingers against the bark, liking the pressure against her tingling nerves. His voice was strange, accented in a way she had never heard. But, what did that matter? She understood his words easily enough. Unnaturally shy, she watched him with wide eyes.

"Come out. I will not hurt you. I promise." He gentled his voice and swung down from his mighty horse. She had never seen a creature so big and thick with muscles. The Forestter men were lean and tall, like the trees that filled her homeland. His horse was huge too. Paige guessed it would have to be to carry such a man as this.

He wore a loose shirt over tighter breeches. Boots laced up his calves, over the pants. A sprinkling of hair exposed through the opened laces of his shirt caught her attention, as did the puckering of a scar. Her eyes lifted to his hair, messed up and accented with bits of the forest. Bright ribbons caught her attention. They fluttered in the breeze like small flags.

"Fairy," she whispered, realizing this must be what the flying pests looked like in their own world, all big and tall. She looked down at her arms. Was she little now? Would she grow wings?

The fairy man lifted his hand to her, drawing her flighty attention back to him. A hint of dark black design showed on his wrist. His fingers curled as if to order her gently from her hiding place.

But nothing about this man appeared to be a fairy pest, beyond his ribboned hair. No, he looked...

Big. Muscled. Strong. Extraordinary. Delectable.

"Fairy?" he repeated, the word softer than the others. "Are you new to my world, my lady?"

Paige nodded, entranced by his lips and the way they opened and closed each time he spoke. Even from the distance she could see the fine texture of their fullness. She wondered if he would let her touch them. Her fingers tapped lightly against the bark. The scent of nature became heady as her breathing deepened.

His beckoning fingers stopped moving and his hand dropped somewhat. Huskier than before, he asked, "Did you come to Fallenrock through the fairy rings?"

Fallenrock? What a curious name.

Again, she nodded. Heat churned inside her, melting her insides and causing her to shake. Every instinct told her she was safe, that he wouldn't hurt her, that she could go to him, that she should go to him.

Go to him.

"I am Sir Aidan of Fallenrock. I promise you, no one will harm you here. You are most welcome, my lady. You are—"

Paige stepped from behind the tree and stood naked before him. Well, naked except for the gauze belt whose ends tickled her thighs when she moved. His words ended abruptly, dying on his still parted lips, as his eyes swooped down and up only to finally land on her breasts. The brown-green orbs lit with an inner magic. She could see it in the way the light reflected in the pools of his eyes. This proved it. He was a fairy after all. It made sense that she would fall for his magic.

She stared back just as intently, taking in the thick cords of his neck, the texture of his skin, the breadth of his shoulders, the tapering line of his waist, the thickness of his legs. That's where her eyes stopped. His weight shifted just enough so she could see the bulge of his erection hinted beneath his shirt. Her desires only increased, as did her curiosity to see more, until she couldn't think or reason beyond the feelings of lust churning inside her. She wanted him. No, she needed him. He was air and food and water and shelter. He was every base need she had ever experienced and she could no more stop her feet from walking toward him than she could give up all those other things.

Go to him. Touch him. Feel him. Breathe him in.

Words were beyond her. He hadn't moved, his hand still unmoving between them, his lips still parted as if frozen in time. Paige didn't try to make sense of what was happening. She went to him, drawn to the texture of his skin, the strength of his body and finally into the heat of his chest. Selfishly, she studied his features up close, not stopping to wonder what he thought or what he wanted. He smelled of fallen leaves and she pressed her cheek along his jaw to breathe him in. As her skin brushed his for the first time, she moaned.

Touch. Feel. More. Breathe.

Paige reached for his neck, running her hands over his tense muscles. He didn't stop her. In fact, he still didn't move. Her fingers traced the scar on his neck before twining in the laces of his shirt.

Touch more.

She ran her fingertips over him. Reaching his waist, she thrust her hands beneath the hem of his shirt, driving them upward onto the naked flesh his stomach and chest. Paige felt small next to him and she was considered tall for her people. Moaning, she explored the defined valleys of his upper body. Every nerve stung with desperation and it showed in the growing roughness of her touch.

"Were you sent for me?" he asked.

Paige barely heard him. But at his expectant look, she nodded—anything to get him to touch her the way she needed him to. Her sex ached, radiating hot desire. He lifted his shirt and tossed it aside, revealing the muscles she had been so apt to explore. Scars marred his skin and the black designs ringing his wrists were repeated higher on his biceps.

More.

He lowered his mouth and kissed her, hard. Paige let him, parting her lips to allow him complete access. The taste of him filled her mouth. His chest pushed fully into her breasts, rubbing the taut nipples. It was unlike anything she had ever felt. Even in her euphoric state, she let him take the lead, bending to the obvious confidence of his embrace. Strong, firm hands slid down her sides, cupping her hips and ass. She was still a little sore from where the fairies slid her ass over the coarse stone, but the pain seemed far away and unimportant. Aidan pressed her against his arousal, rocking so she felt every inch. At any other time she would have been afraid, but the ambrosia didn't allow for fear or prudence.

Must have more. Feel him. Touch him. Breathe him. More.

Paige reached her arms around him and held tight. He walked her back into a tree, holding her up by her ass when she would stumble. The bark scratched her skin, but not so bad she wanted to stop. She clawed frantically at his flesh, scratching in her haste.

Aidan's hands were between them now, jerking at the laces along his hip. When he couldn't free himself fast enough, he growled. The animalistic sound gave her chills. He was as desperate as she.

Even before the pants slid around his hips, he lifted her legs and surged forward. With little effort, he found the entrance to her sex with the thick tip of his cock. Paige's eyes opened wide at the innumerable sensations the touch caused. She looked at Aidan's face, but his eyes were closed tight and his mouth open. Her hands had tangled into his hair, dislodging a ribbon.

More?

She trembled, shaken from the euphoria as her confidence wavered. The intimate press became firm as he thrust up into her. A tiny glint of pain struck her, but the ambrosia-induced tingling soon replaced it, urging her back into the sexual trance until every part of her concentrated on the heat between her thighs. Her body's moisture welcomed him, but the muscles were not so accommodating as they pulsed tightly against the thick intruder. If Aidan noticed, he didn't let on. A light tickle erupted along her clit as Aidan moved. He pumped himself into her, pushing deeper with each pass.

"Ah, this feels so..." His words faded as he moaned in low tones, the sounds almost like words but nothing she could understand.

Paige let it happen, back pressed into a tree and all her senses on fire, not wanting him to stop but unable to do much more than hold on while he claimed her. She clawed at his neck, the ache too much, too hot, too deep. If it didn't end soon, she just knew she would die. Surely no mortal could survive such bittersweet agony.

And then, finally, she found blessed release. Tremors racked over her stomach, sending a burst of energy over her form. Aidan grunted, jabbing a couple more times before going still.

The energy dissipated into the nature around them. Paige felt it go, leaving her relaxed and tired and incredibly warm. The flutter of a bright ribbon caught her attention and she mumbled, "Lovely, lovely fairy, breathe in the beautiful fairy," before falling into a dreamless sleep.

* * *

Aidan caught the woman up in his arms and held tight as her head rolled back on her shoulders. Her chest rose and fell against him in even breaths. Stunned that he had acted with little thought to the consequences, he looked around the forest. They were alone. He lifted her up and carried her around the tree where he had first seen her hand reaching out toward the spider. By the delicate wrist bone, he had known her to be female, but never could he have expected just how womanly she was.

When she stepped in front of him, naked and unashamed, his heart nearly leapt from his chest. One look at her pale skin and he had been bewitched. The supple flesh was completely unmarred but for a long, trailing scar that wound from beneath her armpit to her navel. The scar would be of much envy and reverence, for this woman was a survivor and a great addition to Starian's proud society.

And she was his. All his. A blessing from the gods.

Rich, red waves flowed wildly around her shoulders, as if combed by the wind. And those eyes, so wide and curious, so confident and alluring, deeply green like the fresh grasses of springtime. His cock had lifted as he looked her over and he couldn't turn away. Oh, and how tight she had been, squeezing him in a way he had never felt before with the camp followers who serviced the armies.

He had wished for a wife to come through the fairy rings, had begged the gods to make him worthy of a real bride, not a bartered one. As if by divine intervention, here she was, in his arms, so sweet and accepting, agreeing to be his.

All his.

Aidan grinned and hugged her tighter. He was sure he had never felt so happy—at least not since childhood when he had been entrusted with his first real sword.

The forest ground was clear with no evidence of a fairy ring beyond a flattened circle of grass. He supposed that could be it. Though he had never actually seen a fairy portal, he had always heard the rings were made of mushrooms.

Wherever the woman came from, it was clear she was not from Staria. Women from his world might dress provocatively, but they'd never run around the forest in nothing but a sheer belt. Feeling her warmth, his sated body began to stir once more. The gods had indeed blessed him. With the breeding ceremony so close, the king expecting him to choose a wife and the Oracles of Fallenrock warning he must quickly take a bride or be forever alone, Aidan knew it was none too soon.

Hugging her close, he fought the urge to shout his happiness to the whole village. He couldn't carry her through town for all to see—naked and unconscious. Feeling the tickle of ribbon at his neck, he realized his hair was still ridiculously braided. It only confirmed what he already knew—she was not Starian. A Starian woman would never have ignored such a humorous sight.

Aidan adjusted her in his arms and set to work dressing her in his tunic shirt before angling her limp body over his shoulder to mount his horse. The trained animal stayed steady while he slid her before him. The softness of her pressed tightly to him and when the horse took a step, rocking her gently against his hips, he groaned in pleasure-pain. His desire was far from sated and he thanked the gods the king sent him home to await the breeding ceremony. If he kept her in his house, away from everyone, at least for a while, he would have time to fulfill his passions and hers. Pulling her close, he buried his face in her hair and whispered, "Mine."

2

PAIGE TRIED to open her eyes, but her vision blurred and she was forced to close them to block out the dizzying sight. The smell of the forest engulfed her, warm and earthy, yet sweet as if she lay on a bed of flowers. The sensations that racked her before had yet to wear off and the more aware her mind became of her surroundings, the more the magic of the fairy ambrosia seemed to once more work its way over her flesh.

Was this what it felt like to live in the fairy realm? Sexual need every waking moment? Fiery passions and desperate need?

She moaned, wiggling on the ground. Petals tickled her naked legs though material covered her sensitive breasts and stomach. With the movement, the smell of Aidan replaced the forest. The desire she felt bubbling beneath the surface intensified.

Aidan of Fallenrock. Aidan.

A flood of memory came back to her. Aidan's kiss. His touch. His body inside hers.

Aidan, surely is a prince amongst fairies. Prince Aidan. Handsome prince of the fairies.

Did he give her the shirt she now wore? Would he be there if she opened her eyes? Or would her desires lead her to the next man she saw, fading Aidan as another took his place? Did sex with any man, or rather fairy, feel the same as it had with him? She couldn't imagine how. Then again, from her very limited sexual experiences, she couldn't imagine much.

"I'm here. Methought to wait until the cover of darkness before riding close to town. Methought you might like privacy to—"

"Aidan?" That voice! It sent delicious chills over her. Had she called out to him? She couldn't remember and barely processed anything he said. Things did not seem to move the same in the fairy world. Blindly, her hand searched in the direction of his voice, easily finding warm flesh. She slid her fingers over his naked chest, skimming the hard, small buds of his nipples. He trembled beneath her touch and she smiled. "My prince."

"Hardly a prince." His hand slipped over hers and he lifted a wrist to his mouth. "Merely a knight."

His tongue flickered over her pulse, causing it to race. When she opened her eyes, she saw evening had darkened in the fairy forest. She sought Aidan's face, finding him bent over her arm. The ribbons were gone from his hair and it had been combed and smoothed about his shoulders. A damp lock tickled her arm and she realized he had bathed.

"I did not mean to injure you, my lady." He kissed the tips of her fingers, saying in between caresses, "I found blood. Had I known you were untouched by men I would have been—"

Paige moaned, finding hold in his hair to draw his face down to hers. She parted her lips, unable to think or talk, unable to listen to his words. All she could do was feel and touch. The tingling came back, not as fiery as before, but insistent and very real. The closer Aidan leaned, the hotter she became until cream flooded her sex and the ache of her desire shook her to the bone.

He braced his weight on either side of her, as he gave her the kiss she craved. His tongue dove into her mouth, exploring and tempting. When she moved to return the kiss, he sucked her tongue between his lips. Every movement became a desperate, thoughtless search for completion. She had tasted release once and her body demanded she do so again and again.

Paige clawed at his flesh as her legs sought to entangle his. She found the smooth material of his breeches and wanted to scream in disappointment. She extended her leg until her foot bumped his naked one. Frantic with the ever-growing need, she worked her toes along his calf, trying to grab the tight material of his pants to tug them off.

Heat centered on her breasts, which seemed to radiate and pulse with the sensitive fairy magic. It was the only way to describe the dull pain that settled there. Squirming like a madwoman, she tore at her shirt, finally managing to work it up so that her stomach and breasts were exposed. Aidan grabbed on to her, molding his hand to her chest as he rubbed an aching globe.

Her toes weren't making progress and she groaned. With a strength she didn't know she possessed, she rolled Aidan over onto his back. He gasped in surprise, but didn't stop her from tugging at the laces along his hip. She jerked at his pants, trying to get them off.

"Ow, my lady, hold a moment," he exclaimed, as the tightly fitted material caught on his erection. He took over, pulling the laces free with practiced ease and pushing the material down without doing further injury to his cock.

Paige tossed her shirt aside. Without apology, she lifted above him with a single-minded purpose. She needed him, had to have him. When she guided his stiff arousal to her sex, she nearly screamed at the explosion of pleasure that racked through her entire being.

Paige impaled herself on his thick shaft, ignoring the sore muscles and tight fit as she finally got what she wanted. She kept him deep and circled her hips, exploring the fullness of the penetration.

"You will be the death of me," Aidan exclaimed, gripping her hips tight. He lifted her up only to slam her back down. Paige yelped in surprise at the plethora of sensations the action caused. Pleasure rippled over her, coupled with a driving need for more. When he would stop, she lifted herself back up and did it again.

She braced herself on his chest and her knees on the ground, riding him without thought or care. Nothing mattered beyond the burning desire low in her belly, the deep ache needing to be filled, the instinct to find completion. When she felt her climax nearing, she rocked harder, leaning closer to his chest.

"Ah, ah, oh," Aidan breathed, punctuating each slam of her body to his.

He tensed beneath her, jerking violently as his mouth opened wide. She kept going, closing her eyes tight until finally the tension exploded into a wave of perfect release. Only the tense quivering of her muscles kept her upright. When finally, the tremors lessened, she collapsed onto Aidan's chest. Arms caught her, but she still felt as if she were falling through the very earth beneath them. And before she could utter a single word, sleep claimed her once more.

* * *

Aidan breathed hard, weak from the intensity of his climax. He had never seen a woman ride him quite like...

He frowned. He still hadn't gotten her name. In fact, he hadn't gotten much at all beyond her seemingly insatiable cravings.

She lay against his chest, unmoving, with his cock still imbedded inside her. Had she not so fully slaked his lust, he would have been curious about her behavior. Maybe she had orgasmed so hard she passed out. He knew he had never come quite like that. Then again, maybe the trip through the fairy ring had been rough. Whatever the reason, it didn't matter. They had the rest of their lives to get to know each other and he looked forward to discovering everything. As he ran his hand over her naked back, he groaned.

Everything.

Rolling her over, he gently laid her on the ground. His body slipped from hers and he couldn't help but look at her naked form sprawled beneath him. The ever-darkening sky shadowed them in their own little alcove. Red hair wisped over her face, as if pointing his attention down to her breasts. Cupping one gently, he drew his hand lower, tracing the scar over her stomach to her navel before detouring down to the darker red curls guarding her sex.

By the way she acted, it was quite possible he had been wrong about her maidenhead. It wasn't like he had been with an untouched woman before. Either way, it didn't matter to him. She was his now. No man would ever dare to touch her. He would make sure of it.

Mine.

With the late hour, it would be safe to ride by town under the cover of darkness. Most of the villagers would be finishing their evening meals and settling in for the night. There was little risk of them being seen.

"Rest well, my lady," he whispered, stroking her hair from her face to reveal her delicate features. She made no indication that she heard him. "I will have you home soon enough and there we can properly start our life together. I will honor you and make you proud to be my wife. Together we will have many sons, and if the gods so bless us, a daughter."

ACCURSED, *hateful, spiteful Faerians.*

Paige's head throbbed, each pulse sending a sharp pain down her spine to dissipate throughout her limbs. Once as a young child she had picked a bad mushroom in the forest and chopped it onto the family meal, thinking to be helpful. The hallucinations of dancing tree rats and singing grass blades were nothing compared to what she had just experienced at the hands of those spiteful, fairy-worshiping wenches.

Thankfully, whatever they drugged her with had

run its course and her brain was again her own—even if it pounded like the maydrums of festival. Like she would willingly believe she had fallen through a fairy ring and met up with a handsome, sexy fairy prince lover without first being poisoned. Well, those ladies had their little fun. It was Paige's turn—as soon as she felt up to it. It wasn't like she had anything better to do with her upcoming winter. By the time she finished with the Faerians, they'd think the forest was overrun with ghosts and the priestess would have no choice but to move the fairy worshiping village north, far away from Paige's home.

They drugged the wrong Forestter and they will pay for what they did. I'll make sure of it.

Paige moaned, stretching against the softness cradling her body. She didn't remember grabbing the winter furs for her bed, but she must have because she was lying on them. How exactly did she get home? The Faerians kidnapped her in the hunting forest and didn't necessarily know where she kept her home. She had made a point of cloaking her cabin with trees, rocks and bushes. As a woman living alone, separated from her people, she couldn't be too careful.

And why in the world did her lower stomach feel as if it had been ripped open and crudely sewn back shut? Paige reached for her side, running her hand along the old scar, half expecting her stomach to be ripped apart. Wrenching open one eye and praying the light wouldn't hurt her already pounding head, she frowned. This wasn't her cabin. In fact, this wasn't any place she recognized.

Even in the dark shadows cast with a dying fire, she could see the clay walls were nothing like her wooden ones. It seemed strange to put a fire in the wall. Where she came from, her people had center pits that rose through a hole in the ceiling. Then again, their homes were made of wood and a fire wall would have burned them down.

Where have they taken me? I need to escape.

A small slit on the wall served as a window. There was no way she could slip through the narrow space. Her other option was a door, but who knew what awaited her on the other side?

Did the Faerians keep her?

Finding a wall filled with weapons, her concern deepened. No, this wasn't the Faerians. Fairies were reported to hate all things war and a self-respecting Faerian would never keep a weapon in her home—let alone two dozen displayed on her bedroom wall like trophies of honor.

Had the Faerians sold her?

Paige sat up and her stomach twinged. She pressed the flat of her hand against it, massaging the muscles in tight circles. Forget ripping her apart, she felt as if someone had punched her repeatedly in the gut. A fleeting image of her body being pressed into a tree filtered through her.

"No, surely..." She reached over her shoulder, trying to feel her back. When that didn't work, she lowered her arm and tried reaching behind her waist. The backs of her fingers grazed over a light, burning scrape. "No. That was a dream. It couldn't be real."

Reality hit her hard. Her first time with a man and she did it drugged, with a stranger? Her whole adult life she wondered what it would be like, but none of the men from her tribe would touch her. They thought her cursed like the rest of her family and perhaps they were right. Sure, she pleasured herself whenever the mood struck and had even seen couples in the forest when they thought no one watched.

Was this the man's home? Had he helped her? Decided to keep her? What tribe was he from? She closed her eyes, trying to remember what he looked like—strong muscles, hard skin, scars. "Ribbons."

Ribbons? Paige shivered. No warrior man would dare to wear ribbons unless he hailed from the south.

The Carvers were reportedly insane from years spent deep in caves. But, no, surely not one of them. No one had seen a Carver for decades.

It only left one plausible option. She really did travel through the fairy ring. She followed the memory of his face, forcing her brain to concentrate. As recollections trickled to the forefront of her thoughts, she remembered him mentioning the rings.

A creak sounded and she jolted in alarm, tugging the fur up to cover her naked body. The man fairy appeared in the doorway, though he had no ribbons or wild braids. His long, blond hair had been combed smooth and left to hang about his shoulders. In fact, he wore nothing at all.

Paige clamped her legs together, almost unable to breathe. The memory of her release was not lost to her, but the pounding, wanton acts to get there came with it. Her eyes rounded and she looked at his naked cock. By its aroused state it became clear what he thought she would do for him. But the wanton, ambrosia-laced Paige was gone. She hugged the fur tighter.

"You are awake, my lady." The husky tone sent a shiver down her spine. What she wouldn't give for her bow and quiver of arrows. He glanced down his body before giving her a lopsided grin. "Methought to make it easier for us this time."

This time? Paige opened her mouth to speak, but only a squeak came out. How did she answer such an assumption? How did she answer a naked man at all? She tried to push the fur into her skin until it became so lodged he would never be able to rip it off.

"I wish to take you slower, so that I may touch and taste every inch of your body. It will be a pleasure to explore you." He stepped closer and his erection only grew.

Paige lifted up her hand, finally managing to eek out, "One moment, there, Sir, ah, Fairy. Whatever you think is going to happen is, ah, well, not going to happen."

"Sir Fairy?" His smile fell and the playful light died in his eyes. "I am Sir Aidan of Fallenrock. Do you not remember me? I am the man you came through the rings to find."

"I somewhat remember you," she offered weakly. "It's been a really long, strange, *very* strange day. I'm afraid I haven't been myself and you might have gotten the wrong impression about me."

"No, I understand perfectly, my lady. You have no reason to worry. I will honor you and make you proud. I officially spoke the word. I chose you for mine."

"For your what?"

"The gods had the fairies send you to me to be my bride. When you arrived, you said it was so and I have claimed you as my wife, my lady. Do not worry. It is done."

Wife? My lady? Done?

I'm in trouble.

Danger, Paige. The man fairy is delusional.

"I am not a lady," she said, her voice not as strong as she would have liked. "I am not of noble birth."

"All women in Staria are ladies, from the fisherman's wife to Queen Patricia," he assured her. "And you are *my* lady."

"I might have been fairy drugged, but I'm pretty sure I'd remember two fortnights filled with no-touch intention courting and the exchanging of blood to seal a union." Just in case, she looked at her arm to be sure it wasn't cut. The skin was smooth. Even if it wasn't, she definitely remembered there being a lot of touching going on. If it would have been possible, she would have clamped her legs even tighter.

"That must have been the custom from your world." He nodded and seemed to relax, as if understanding her confusion over their shared situation.

"Here, in Staria, the man simply has to state it is so and a woman becomes his bride. Because we are always at war, it is necessary to make the most of the life we have. Often, there is no time for so much stating of intentions before marrying." Then he laughed. "And we definitely would not go two full fortnights without touching our wives should they be near enough to touch."

"You're always at war?" What the devil was happening here? She looked at the weapons wall. How could he be a fairy if he went to war and had knives in his home? "You're not a fairy, are you?"

"I am mortal. We do not have fairies in our land. It is said they do not appreciate wars and so stay away." He stepped closer, so close she could have touched him had she felt the need to reach out. She gripped the fur tighter still. "We only find the gifts they send us from the gods to reward us for serving well in battle. You are my gift."

Paige tried to inch her way toward the wall without being too noticeable. It was hard with his brown-green eyes piercing into her, watching her every breath. With the intent of keeping him talking and distracted, she asked, "And who exactly are you at battle with?"

"The Caniba, a horrible race of snake people

who live in the ground and eat the flesh of men. We have fought with them since the beginning of written time and we will always fight until the last one is dead." His gaze narrowed in distraction.

"Sounds more like a tale to scare children," she mused. *That's it, just a little more, almost there. Keep him talking. Get a weapon.*

"They are no child's tale. The Caniba are very real," he assured her. "It is told to children that our enemies are beasts, a race born of the unholy fornications of people and wolves. I have killed many to know they are of flesh and blood, but the Caniba are the lowest possible form a man can become."

Aidan reached for the wall and took down a knife. Flipping it around in his palm with practiced ease, he offered her the hilt. "You may have it and others if it makes you feel better, but we are far north of the borderlands. And I promise you I will protect you with my life. You have no reason to fear. You are safe."

Paige's hand trembled. She had not distracted him for a moment. He knew she reached for a weapon and offered it freely, completely unconcerned with what she might do with it. She reached to take the short knife, feeling only slightly better now that she held it in her grasp.

Paige did her best to look at his face, consciously keeping her gaze from wandering down his body. A small tingle erupted inside her, not like the rush of ambrosia but a normal, feminine reaction to a handsome man—who just happened to be standing naked and aroused before her as if any second she would stop talking and invite him into her bed. For the life of her, she didn't even know how to do such a thing without dying of embarrassment. Heat rushed over her face at the very idea. "So... what? The gods send you a woman and you just decide to love and marry her just like that? No conversation? No careful consideration?"

That's right, Paige, keep him talking until you can think of how to get out of this.

"Love?" He arched a brow. "I do not believe I said anything about such nonsense. I have heard it told that many of the women sent to us by the fairies speak of romantic love being a reason to join. Such is not our way. It is hoped a union will produce affection and, more importantly, a vessel for sexual release and pleasure."

"Why marry at all?" She fingered the blade gingerly. Her jaw tightened at the idea of being called a mere vessel to fuck, as she uttered, "If all you need is a vessel then why not find a willing woman of low morals? Or have they all been claimed by other men?"

"The gods smile at our unions and once we marry, we do not seek another. We stay faithful because the gods demand discipline. War demands discipline. Marriage is not based on love. It is need. A man needs a woman to give him children, to cook and look after his home when he is gone to battle. And, in return, the woman is given a place to live, food and protection."

How romantic, she thought sarcastically.

"I see." Paige should have been shouting to the heavens in relief at his words. It would have been much worse, and a little creepy, if this stranger professed to love her unconditionally. Instead, his logic was calm and reasonable. Marriage out of necessity. It wasn't an unheard of concept. Many people married because they didn't have much of a choice, though it was usually ill-tempered men who no one else wanted and useless women who were bad with tools and couldn't survive on their own. "But I think I'm going to have to decline your generous offer. New world or not, I can take care of myself. The forest will provide everything I need. It feels like spring, so that gives me what? At least a full season before winter sets in? I can have an adequate home built by then and, so long as the hunting is good, enough food stocked to last me. In the end, I suppose one forest is as good as any other to call home. So, I unspeak the words. This marriage is undone."

There. That should take care of it.

It wasn't like she had a bunch of friends or family waiting for her. Paige bit her lips. She might have to "borrow" a few tools to get the job done, but she would make it work.

His jaw stiffened visibly for a long moment, but then he began to laugh. "My lady likes to play games." Aidan pressed his knee onto the bed. The angle of his body gave her full view of his naked form and showcased the towering member between his legs. "You wish for me to convince you I am man enough to keep you. I am ready to meet your challenge."

"Ah no, I really don't." She tugged at the fur, but his knee had pressed into it and held it tight to the bed. "You said we are away from the battlefront. My people are Forestters. I will be fine on my own. I have been for years."

"That is your name, my lady? Forestter?"

"Paige of the Forestters," she answered absently. Paige tugged harder on the covers.

"Now that you are mine you are to be called Lady Paige of Fallenrock." The playful light didn't leave his handsome gaze. He thought she jested. Aidan slowly licked his bottom lip, drawing her eyes to it. "My very beautiful lady wife."

"Thank you, but no thank you." She tried to sound firm, but with him on the bed the room suddenly felt too small and devoid of air. Paige was running out of ideas. She had never been in this situation before. Sure, she had fought off men who'd invaded her hunting ground, and argued with the old hags who came to purify her of her curse until they left crying and screaming. But this man hunted her body and, by the look on his face and the sexual memories becoming ever clearer in her head, what he had in mind definitely wasn't pure.

"I invoke the law of tribal council and demand my plea be heard," she blurted, desperate.

"We have no such law or council." He licked his lip again. Curse him.

Keep him talking. Make him concentrate on something else until that look is out of his eyes.

"Then what laws do you have for the settlement of disputes?" Was the room getting hotter? Did he lean closer? She resisted the urge to fan her flushed cheeks.

"The highest-ranking man hears the complaint and passes a binding judgment." When he leaned closer, she could smell the subtle hint of what had to be soap on his skin. "With my position in the military, I am the highest-ranking man. Lord Valt of Fallenrock leads armies against the Caniba and has not been home for many, many years."

"Then I demand a second decision! It is not fair for you to judge a situation you are in." Paige's tone rose, not out of anger so much as desperation and a touch of fear.

"No one will dispute my claim. Here in Staria, once a decision is made, it is done. There is no point in making a decision if only to rethink it. You have no Starian husband and, even if you did, I would only have to seek his permission to be a second husband. With my standing, I would not be denied. If you had a husband before coming to this world, he does not matter anymore. The gods knew he was not the one for you. You didn't have a husband, did you?"

"No," she dismissed following with a question of her own. "You said second husband?" Paige gulped. Was this day getting worse? "I'm going to be plagued with more of you, running around and claiming I'm married to them?" Then, under her breath, she muttered, "I'd be better off being a woman of low morals, for at least then I'd be paid and then left alone."

Cursed Faerians!

That statement killed some of his good humor. Paige wondered if he realized he was talking to her naked. Then she wondered if he walked around naked in his home all the time. There was talk of a tribe far, far south of her homeland that never wore clothing. Ever. Her eyes began to trail down his chest once more, but she caught herself and again stared at his intense eyes. She wasn't sure which direction was worse.

"Multiple husbands are only out of necessity. I have land, property, rank and honor. There is no need for us to allow another into our marriage. I can provide for you on my own." Was that jealousy in his voice? He had only known her what? One day at best? With the fairy euphoria, it was a little hard to tell for sure how much time exactly had passed since coming through the ring.

"And I can provide for myself," she insisted. "Whatever you think happened between us, you need to know I was drugged by the fairies—well, by the fairy-worshiping wenches who kidnapped me. If I said or did anything that made you think I agreed to be your wife, I am sorry, but surely even you with

your stern 'decisions are decisions' speech can understand that I am not—"

Aidan surged forward and kissed her. For a
second, her fingers loosened on the fur and she
gasped at the hard yet gentle way he consumed her
mouth. Her lips parted. However she didn't return
the kiss—not because she didn't want it, but because
she had never wanted anything more. Without the
ambrosia urging her uncontrollably on, she had time
to think and feel, to savor and fear.

When he stopped, he didn't pull away and his
lips brushed hers as he spoke. "You did much to
convince me and I would have you do much again.
We are a good match. The gods chose well."

Her stomach tensed, reminding her just how sore
it was. Even if she was brave enough to give in and
act the wanton fool, her body wouldn't be able to take
it. Mumbling the first thing she could think of, she
said, "You hurt my belly. I cannot."

His eyes narrowed and he instantly let go of her.
He sat back on the bed, his face paling at her words
as if she had slapped him. For a long moment, he
didn't move, barely breathed. Aidan looked to her
stomach and then down at his cock, clearly understanding what she meant. To her great surprise, he
stood and strode to the door. He nodded once, not

meeting her eyes again as he stared past her to the wall. "I will leave you to rest."

Stunned, Paige didn't move from her place on the bed as the door shut firmly behind him. Her words had actually stopped him. "Kiss my toes, that really worked."

3

AIDAN DIDN'T COME BACK that night. Though tired, Paige's mind wouldn't let her sleep as she stared at the bedroom door. She wasn't so foolish as to run away in the middle of the night without a stitch of clothing, into unknown woods with unknown creatures. Besides, that would require her to run naked through an unknown house first. After seeing the heat blazing in Aidan's eyes, she knew dashing about naked in front of him was the worst possible plan.

Strange that she should leave her homeland where no man wanted her, to a place where she could potentially have several husbands. Paige supposed she should have been more shaken by her trip through the ring, but it's not like magic was unheard of in her life. She herself was "cursed". Paige always thought her grandmother exaggerated the stories she told of falling through the fairy ring, coming from a land filled with giant square homes called apartments and men who shifted into cats and back again as easy as breathing. It was from her grandmother that Paige and her father had gotten their gifts, or rather her family curse.

When her eyes did wander from the door, she had time to study the room. The firelight died slowly in the square fire box, fading the walls from a brighter orange to a darker brown. The weapons on the wall were well crafted and clearly dominated the room's décor. A few personal toiletries lined a low table in the corner—a comb, an empty bowl and pitcher. All were plain, made more for function than beauty. The last piece of furniture was a wooden trunk at the end of the bed. It was small and she hadn't noticed it when she awoke to find the naked man striding into her room ready to copulate.

A chill worked over Paige each time she thought of it. Aidan had been so proud and carefree in his nakedness without the burden of modesty. And why should he be modest? A man like him, so strong and defined, would know his body and his beauty. By the scars, she believed him when he said he he a fighter. The warrior aspect made her nervous. She had met plenty of fighting men in her forest and they were a stubborn, self-assured lot to deal with. And the men who had a cause? They were the worst. Killing Canibas and following the will of his gods apparently were Aidan's causes in life. If he believed something to be true, for example his marriage to a preordained bride, he would be hard pressed to change his mind about it and even harder pressed to let her go.

Logic told her there was only one way out of this situation. She would have to run, preferably out of Staria to the Caniba side of things. In war, each side hated the other and said nasty things. Paige wondered if the Caniba were so bad as the man-eating beasts Aidan described. If she stayed in this new world, she definitely wanted to see for herself.

If she stayed? Paige laughed wryly. Unless she found a fairy ring to jump through, she was staying. Even then, there was no way of telling where the fairy ring she found would take her. She might end up in a boiling lake or in the world of demons.

As the sun peeked through the window, Paige pushed up from the bed and tried to look out over the land. Not surprising, she only saw trees beyond an empty clearing. She went to the trunk. A few pieces of clothing filled it, all clearly meant for Aidan. They smelled of him, which only brought back the sexual rush she had been trying hard to suppress.

Cursed fairy magic. Cursed Faerians.

Out of the whole situation, her loss of control upset her most. Had she had her wits about her, she could have faced Aidan logically and reasonably, stopping him before he came to the conclusion they were destined to be together.

Knowing a stolen shirt was better than a fur blanket, Paige slipped it over her head. The pants were too big, even with the laces on the sides pulled tight. But after a few triangular cuts along the waist, combined with holes poked with the blade tip, she was able to add two more rows of laces in the front and back.

Quite pleased with her handiwork, Paige "borrowed" a knife and tiptoed barefoot from the room. Outside the door she encountered only silence. Window slits in the wall illuminated the sparsely decorated room, revealing a large wooden table and chairs. A barren fire box dominated the wall on the far side of the large rectangular room.

One direction appeared to lead deeper into the house to a row of closed doors. In the other, she saw a narrow stroke of pale, outside light peeking along the bottom seam of a doorway. Paige instantly chose to walk in the direction of freedom, eagerly breathing in the fresh air as she slipped from the house.

A narrow rock-lined path disappeared into the woods beyond the clearing. Paige ignored it, opting for a more rugged escape where she could disappear into the trees. Snaking around the front of the house, she noted how big it was, stretching a half-pacing strike in front of her. Paige's own home barely took up an eight of a strike.

"Come for your morn exercise?"

Paige stiffened, her breath catching in her throat. The sound came from the back of the house and for a moment she could pretend the question wasn't for her.

Aidan slid around the back corner, confronting her. His naked chest glistened from whatever exercise he had found himself engaged in. Hair slicked back from his face, revealing each hard plane of his face, from the bold set of his nose to the shiver-inducing pierce of his eyes. Firm lips brought up the all-too-recent memory of his kiss.

"I see you brought a knife." He glanced meaningfully toward her hand where she gripped the hilt, holding the blade in front of her in a protective gesture. "Do you wish to join me in training? Or are you off to the Hanging Forest to hunt?"

MICHELLE M. PILLOW

"Hanging Forest?" Paige glanced at the trees.

Seeing her apprehension, he said, "It is only a name—nowadays anyway."

"Oh."

"You have come to train with me, then?" He stopped walking when the blade tip neared his stomach. With one thrust, she could have killed him but he was completely unafraid.

"No. I—I..." Paige shook her head in denial. She lifted the hilt and offered it to him. He took it, tossing it toward the ground without looking to make sure it landed. It did, poking from the earth at a sharp angle.

"Or are you too sore?" He didn't move, didn't flinch. Somehow, Paige knew he had suspected her attempt to leave him and wasn't worried by it.

"Sore? No, the bed was comfortable enough —oh." She grabbed her stomach, looking down as if something might suddenly jump out of it. "Um."

Suddenly, he was close, shadowing the light as he towered over her. Aidan placed a hand on the side of the house, leaning so her back was forced against the hard stone. He reached, as if to touch her cheek, and then paused. "Your passion overwhelmed me, but I will be much gentler next time. It had been a long time for me, but I will not lose my head again."

"Next time?" The words squeaked awkwardly

out of her throat. Paige knew how he could make her feel, but without the fairy magic urging her on, how did she give or accept such an offer?

Her heart sped and she wondered if perhaps he planned on that time being now. His eyes definitely said he wanted her, as they boiled with hot emotions. His restrained fingers flexed, so close to her face she felt their heat tingling into her nerves. Through the corner of her vision, she saw the designs etched into his flesh, as much a part of him as his skin. Paige didn't move. Whatever he expected, she could not be the wanton temptress who jumped at the very sight of him. The fairy magic was gone, leaving Paige embarrassed and nervous with memories of what she would never be able to be again. "The fairy magic wasn't me. I was drugged with ambrosia."

"It felt like you." Aidan's fingers glanced along her neck, skating a direct path from her ear to her shoulder, only to stop when he reached the edge of the stolen shirt. "Firm yet soft, warm and wet, so sweet."

The words sent chills over her, creating a liquid warmth between her thighs. She clamped her legs tight. How did she respond to such a thing? Men never talked to her like that. Sure, a few looked, but none dared to touch her.

"You don't want to be with me." She swallowed, hard. "I am cursed."

"Cursed?" He arched a brow, looking more amused than scared. Apparently, the word didn't hold the same meaning here as it did back home. "Tell me, can I help with that affliction, my lady?"

"It is not a game." Paige frowned at his light-hearted treatment of her family shame. Trying to make him understand, she said, "It is going to rain tonight."

Aidan glanced at the clear sky, unconcerned. "This is Fallenrock. We're near the sea cliffs. It rains almost every night." Then, lowering his voice, he leaned closer still. "It is said that the night is when the sea gods come out to play, throwing the waves up over the sides of the cliffs."

Paige felt the whisper of his breath on her lips, caressing her and causing her mind to focus on each unsettled nerve. Fine, if he wasn't impressed with that prediction, she would look for something else. Then see how fast he took back his words about their intertwined fates.

Closing her eyes, she tried to focus even as a large part of her resisted. She didn't want to see, had worked hard to block out what she could never help or control. The cold chill of water splashed over her skin, shivering her to the core. She felt the rocks more than saw them as the wind carried her along the cliffs, past a quickly changing sky. Light turned to darkness and rain. A sea storm raged and her mind became pinned to the rocks before getting sucked into the water. The image of a watercraft being tumbled against the waves hit her and she felt sickened by the turbulent motion. Moonlight caressed an old, weathered hand as it latched onto a rope. The water lurched, tossing the craft onto its side. Wood cracked and splintered, instantly swallowed by the angry ocean.

She opened her eyes, ignoring the discomfort of saying what she saw out loud in the hopes that it would scare him away as it had others. "The storm over the water will be rough. An older man from a coastal village will be taken by the waves tonight when his watercraft is smashed into rocks within ten strikes from here."

Aidan frowned, withdrawing. There. That was the reaction she was used to.

"Did you see his face? What did the boat look like?" he asked.

Now it was Paige's turn to frown. That was *not* the reaction she was used to getting. "No face, just an older hand with a jagged scar across the back." She drew her finger over her hand to show where the mark had been. "And on the boat, there were long beams with rope, but no sides to the craft, just a flat bottom. That craft never had a chance against the sea's wrath."

"That is an old fisherman's boat. It shouldn't be hard to find the owner. Not too many are made like that anymore," Aidan stated. "I had planned on keeping you to myself for a while, but if what you see is true, we must ride to the village center and warn the fisherman. What he does with the knowledge will be his decision."

"You want me to go to the village right now?" Paige began to shake her head in denial. She did not want to face a town full of people, all those eyes on her, judging her for what she saw and for the fact she could see the future at all. "I do not, ah—"

"Not at this exact moment." His tone lowered, drawing her attention back to him. "We have time before we must ride. The rains will not come for many, many hours and the fisherman won't leave port until evening. It will be easier to find him when the village is ripe with activity. With a distinct scar and old boat, it will only take a few moments to locate who you saw."

She found herself nodding in agreement with

him, all of her senses reaching out to him. He smelled of power and strength—an intoxicatingly raw scent of man. It called to her on the most primal of levels. Her nerves tingled with the overwhelming potency of his nearness. The look in his eyes was unmistakable, as was the way his breathing deepened. Paige could think of nothing else, but the virile man growing more dangerous and alluring by the moment.

She tried to tell herself to run, far and long, to escape the passion snapping the air between them like lightning. It connected them somehow, a strange feeling she didn't care to explore. Paige tried to blame the fairies' ambrosia, but she knew that poison had already left her. Whatever happened now was all her.

There was something about him that made her want to throw caution to the wind and act the part of the animal, surviving on pure instinct, fulfilling each animalistic need as it arose.

"I wish to kiss you, my sweet lady," he whispered, the words hoarse and low and incredibly alluring. Paige parted her lips, unable to stop herself. Logic and reason left her and all the excuses in the world couldn't make her stop what they were doing. "I want to taste you."

She panted and his lips caught her breath into

him. The soft kiss sent a thick wave of awareness throughout her body, arousing her until she wanted to scream with desperate need. His tongue circled her lips, tracing around the outer edge, just as her body wanted his cock to trace her most intimate opening. With her eyes closed, she could practically imagine what it would feel like to have him there, thrusting hard into her wet pussy.

"Feel how ready I am for you. Feel how hard my cock is." Aidan moaned, the sound begging her to let him fuck her. To prove his words, he rocked his hips forward, bending his knees to rub his cock into her sensitive stomach. Her back fell against the side of the house, keeping her from falling. "I promise to go slow, to not take you too hard. But I must be inside you, my lady. I ache to find my release, to feel your release as you ride me."

Paige tried to speak, but she couldn't force much more than a squeak from her tight throat. How did she say yes to such a thing? How did she tell this man, this delusional man who claimed they were married, that she wanted him to take her right then and there? What kind of a message would that send? Already he thought she was his wife. What would happen if she said yes to his lust? To her lust? To the very delicious way his cock rubbed into her stomach?

He moaned, as if he could hear every one of her thoughts and was frustrated by them. As if to convince her, his hands began to move, pressing her hard to the side of the house while they explored everywhere they could reach. Fingers tangled in her hair, gripped her waist, glided along her arms and hips, before finally reaching to make quick work of ridding her of her breeches. He tugged at her shirt, lifting it just enough so his breeches pressed into her naked flesh.

"Ah," Paige gasped as the breeze hit her naked thighs. The word "yes" threatened to escape and she pressed her lips tightly together. She prayed she was able to maintain some sort of decency, but the thought was met with a deep, mocking, inner laughter. How was standing alongside a house, trying not to moan, while the most delectable man she had ever seen said he wanted to fuck her, even close to decent?

Before she knew what she was doing, her hips moved forward to meet his, feeling the intimate outline of his arousal along her exposed sex. Her fingers glided around his waist to squeeze his muscular ass and pull him closer. It felt too good and she found herself controlling his hips in her desperation, forcing them forward. She freed her foot from the fallen pants and lifted a leg to rub along his, spreading her thighs to him.

"This is wrong." She tried to be reasonable, but it was hard. "We should stop. We're strangers. You cannot really think we're married."

"You know you were meant for me. The gods sent you to me." He breathed into her ear, the sound raw with desire. "This is not wrong. It is natural and right. You are my wife."

He seemed so sure and his confidence made her less so. She would never be able to justify what she was feeling out loud, but a deep sense of under-standing washed through her. Or perhaps it was just a deep sense of lust. Either way, it overpowered her and she found herself nodding in agreement.

Every nerve reached for him, tingling for contact. She couldn't fight it any longer. She needed release. Her fingers became frantic as she clawed at his clothes. Aidan reached for his breeches, undoing them to free his cock.

Leaning into her, he devoured her neck with kisses before licking a hot trail over her throat to nibble at her ear. He gripped her hips, lifting both of her legs as he pressed her into the wall. Paige cried out in pleasure at the show of strength. The man overwhelmed her. His muscles bulged beneath her hands, flexing and moving with each jerky movement.

Tiny eruptions worked from her pussy through her stomach to her breasts, hardening her nipples beneath her shirt until every little stroke felt like pure torture. Her hands fumbled to touch him, eager to discover if he was as big as she remembered. She took his hard shaft in her hand to feel his enormous length. Even as her pussy grew impossibly moist, she whispered, "This is insanity. This isn't happening."

"Do you want me to stop?" He pulled back, his eyes tortured by the very idea. "I would never force you."

Paige shook her head in denial. She let go of his cock and clung to his shoulders as he adjusted her hips to find aim. If he stopped now, she really would go crazy. Her body was on fire for him, her sex drenched. Maybe her reaction to him wasn't all of the fairies' doing.

Low, primal noises escaped him as he drew the mushroomed tip of his cock along her slick folds. He bumped her clit, causing her to buck up. The side of the house scratched at her back but she didn't care. His cock glided to her moist center, finding her pussy soaked with the cream of her body. He buried his face close to her neck as he thrust up.

Aidan rocked. Her pussy convulsed with pleasure, tightening around him. He leaned back to study her face. A relieved grin crossed over his devilish features. The long length of his hair blew back from his shoulders, adding a wild appeal to the warrior before her.

Holding her with ease, he did not ask permission again as he moved within her. He went slowly at first, in and out, in and out. Her legs wrapped him, urging him to go harder with each pass. As he obeyed the silent command, she cried out in pleasure. The natural rhythm of his hips quickened.

Aidan answered her with a loud grunt. Losing all control, he drove himself forward, only to pull out and do it again, conquering her fully. Tension worked its way over her, centering on her hips. With each thrust he pounded deeper and she was sure he might rip her in half.

But oh, what a way to go.

She held onto him, helpless to do anything but ride out the bittersweet ecstasy of pleasure. Paige gasped loudly several times before softly moaning as an orgasm racked her body. Aidan slowed but didn't stop. He rode out her release. As the tremors subsided, he groaned and seated himself deep. He jerked violently, his body exploding inside her.

Their trembling aftermath continued for what felt like both an eternity and an instant. Slowly, he lowered her to the ground. Her legs felt like they were weighted with steel cuffs. Kissing her gently, he looked into her eyes as if he would never let go.

But he did let go. The tenderness she saw vanished as quickly as it came. Paige eyed him, insecurely searching for a sign of something—of what exactly she wasn't sure. It wasn't as if she expected words of love or even mild affection. When he didn't readily speak, she said awkwardly, "We should leave."

Not that I really want to go to the village.

"Of course. I will be but a moment." Aidan patted her arm, appearing distracted, before rushing toward the front of the house.

Paige watched him, stunned. Though she wasn't sure what shocked her more—the fact they'd just had sex and he acted as if nothing transpired, or that when she told him about her vision, he didn't look at her like she had lost her wits. Aidan accepted what she said, no questioning or fear, and acted. She turned her attention to the nearby forest. If she ran, she could hide in the trees. He would never find her, not if she didn't want to be found.

She couldn't move her feet. What if this vision was different? What if the fisherman was saved?

"Do you ride?" Aidan asked.

Paige blinked, realizing he had come back while she was lost in thought. He had put on a fresh tunic shirt and had slicked back his hair with water. Frantically, she reached to the ground to pull on her pants. When he approached, she detected the faint hint of forest herbs on him. "I run. Where I live I can't afford to keep a horse through winter. You do mean a horse, right? Or did you mean a cart?"

Aidan smiled slightly, striding toward the back of the house, motioning her to follow him. She did, lacing her pants as she walked. He reached down to grab the knife, wiping it on the inside of his tunic before slipping it into a sheath along his upper thigh. "Methinks our worlds were not so different. I am very glad. It means you will be comfortable here. Some women who have come through the rings speak of strange contraptions that, for all I can understand, only encourage laziness. They take longer to find their happiness in Staria for they are not used to doing for themselves. I have heard tales of a woman who stared at a fire pit yelling at it to feed her because in her world she merely had to demand her needs from a magical cooking box."

"How many worlds are there?"

"Countless. We have no way of knowing the number, though there are those who say the worlds go on forever. For all I know, you came from across the ocean, from a land I've never heard of right on this planet." Aidan led her across the back clearing, toward a long, stone building. From the width and height of the doorway, she deduced it was his stables. "To tell the truth, other than waiting for you to fall through the fairy rings, I have not pondered the other worlds too much. The only reality that matters is this one—ours."

Paige waited for him outside as he disappeared into the building. Aidan seemed so sure of their shared fate. He truly believed the fairies sent her to him and that they would live the rest of their lives together. Sure, today the thought might be tempting, even tomorrow—especially when her bones still felt like liquid and her heart still fluttered in remembrance of his touch. But what about after the newness of discovery wore off when he learned she kept to her own schedule? When she disappeared for days, beholden to none, just so she could sleep beneath the trees and stars? Even if she could recapture the passionate confidence of the fairy magic, reality would find its way in.

He returned, leading a horse to where she stood. "This is not how I would spend your first day in our home."

Our home. Paige couldn't meet his gaze. This wasn't her home. She had no home thanks to the Faerians.

"But if you have the gift of the oracles, we cannot ignore what you saw." He touched her cheek, forcing her to look at him. "Now, more than ever, I am confident the fairies sent you to the right place. Fallenrock is home to all oracles and I vow to protect that gift, lady wife."

Lady wife. Oracles. Gift. Paige screamed silently at herself for not running when she had the chance.

"Come, you'll ride with me until we can get you your own mount." He cupped his hands, indicating she should hop up onto the large animal's back.

She did, swinging her leg up and over as she grabbed the beast's mane. On instinct, she nudged its side, trying to race it forward and away. The horse lurched, but a quick command and tug of the reins by Aidan stopped the animal from darting off.

"We will have to teach you to ride as well." Seating himself behind her, he wrapped an arm about her waist and pulled her tight to his chest. Fire erupted along her back, trailing its flame through her blood to center over her chest and thighs. Lowering his voice, he whispered along her neck. "You're shivering. There is no reason to be frightened of the villagers. They will rejoice in your coming as I have."

AIDAN WAS glad that his wife's face was turned from him because he couldn't quit grinning like a fool. As easily as he could accept the will of the gods, he still found amazement in the fact that they'd so thoroughly answered his prayers. Not only was Lady Paige beautiful and soft and full of passion for him, she had the gift of sight. As an oracle, she was exactly where she belonged—away from the borderlands and the reach of the Caniba. Here, the people of Fallenrock would guard her secret with their lives. In fact, they guarded all oracles so fiercely that a large part of Starian society didn't even know the seers existed.

The steady gait of his horse rocked the couple as they took the easiest path through the forest. Trees surrounded them, the leaves crashing their music as the limbs protected the travelers from the high breeze. He hugged her tighter and she stiffened.

"Do you worry for the fisherman?" He worked his fingers along her stomach, massaging her while keeping her close. Her words about his hurting her stung. He hadn't meant to treat her roughly. Women were to be protected, not harmed. In fact, he wasn't sure it was exactly his doing. Hadn't she been the aggressor those first times?

Still, I should have resisted her. I should have taken better care with such a delicate creature.

Ignoring what he thought might be her resistance to him as the paranoia of a new husband, he stayed on course. Naturally, there would be an adjustment as they learned each other's moods, but this marriage was meant to be, ordained by the gods in reward of his loyalty, valor and sacrifice. He had lost his family to the battlefield, leaving him with little more than an empty house, old memories and a mother who'd taken to the sea to both escape suitors and reality.

But Paige would change that. She represented the future. Together they would fill their house with sons and the walls would no longer echo the deafening silence. With her arrival, he felt hope. She saved him from facing the Divinity otherworlders and she would save him from the lonely emptiness. The gods decreed it. How could it be any other way? Their joined destiny was as sure to him as the surrounding trees and rocks.

Aidan took a deep breath, trying not to smell her

hair as it tickled his face. His cock had been half aroused since sliding behind her on the horse, even after she allowed him to take her against the house. Surely she felt it, knew how he wanted her again, how he ached to carry her off into the forest and make love to her under the dancing shade of the trees.

Finally, after a long silence, she answered, "I don't hold out much hope of saving the people I see, any more than I can control the weather that's coming to take them away."

THE SOUND of waves crashing over rocks could be heard long before Paige saw the expansive ocean reaching out over the distance near the bottom of a steep incline. At first, it was hard to block out the water, even as the sounds of Fallenrock Village grew in volume. A long dirt and rock street led through the center of town, flat and well looked after. On either side, small homes sprawled out into the distance. They were constructed from the same material as Aidan's but were much smaller in design.

Young boys played in the yards and along the street, swinging sticks, knocking over planters and yelling words of mock battle. No one paid the lads any attention, as if their mischief were part of any regular day. Only when they started calling out to Sir Aidan, inquiring about the woman on his horse, did the townsfolk actually look up to see what the commotion was about.

The farther they rode, the more houses gave way to tightly set structures. Strange smells wafted over what Aidan called the center square, flavoring the air with odd herb combinations as they passed cooking meats and breads. A large, carved hole in the middle of the square had steps winding down into the earth. People appeared from within carrying pitchers of water. They stopped to look at her, joining the growing crowd that now blocked the road.

The women eyed her clothing and frowned, whispering amongst themselves. They all wore dresses—long skirts and bodices so tight they nearly squeezed their womanly charms up and out of the low-cut necklines. How a woman could work, let alone breathe in such a contraption, was beyond Paige's imagination.

The men, though rough in appearance, wore clean clothes much like the ones Aidan donned. Tunic shirts in light-colored fabrics hung loose over tighter breeches. Many wore no shirt at all, instead showing off bare chests bronzed by the sun. From young to old, they appeared healthy and muscled and some of them were practically gigantic. Scars lined their bodies, attesting to a hard life. All but the boys and women had black bands around their upper arms and a few even had wrist markings like Aidan.

If she had doubts, this town confirmed she wasn't home. The men of her village were tall and slender, made for running through the trees while shooting a bow. Only the tales of the Carvers could match the breadth and height of these men, though Starians clearly lacked the wild lunacy of that race.

"Tell them what you saw," Aidan urged her, his breath tickling the back of her ear.

Paige stiffened fully, if that was even possible since she had been rigid from the moment he had slid behind her on the horse. She shook her head in jerky denial. The last time she had been in front of a crowd of villagers there had been talk of stoning her for "bringing on the wrath of Sister Nature".

"This is my bride, Lady Paige, sent by the fairies to Fallenrock because she is an oracle," Aidan announced. The words were met with a rush of excited chatter. A group of young boys lifted their stick swords, pumping them in the air.

"Hand me your knife, Aidan," she whispered out

of the side of her mouth, reaching around to Aidan's thigh. He placed his hand over hers, stopping her from finding it. Apparently, the townsfolk weren't so keen on the idea of another oracle. She twisted her hand in the horse's mane, ready to ride—with or without Aidan on the back.

"Rejoice!" an old man with a weathered face and raspy voice called from the crowd, the word lifting above the others. Paige jolted in alarm. "Rejoice! Sir Aidan has chosen."

"Rejoice! Rejoice!" Shouts joined the first, growing and floating over the distance. "Sir Aidan has chosen a wife! The new oracle is his wife!"

A sudden panic filtered through Paige. Her eyes darted over the crowd, seeing their smiling faces looking up at them. They stepped forward, moving as one mass to press in upon the new couple. A hand brushed her calf and she automatically lifted her knee to get away. She pressed into Aidan's chest, trying to climb up onto the horse's back. His hand snaked around her waist, holding her steadily to his hard frame. A shiver worked over her, but the sensation barely registered. After living in the forest by herself, she didn't like all this direct attention.

"Back," Aidan commanded. He was met with instant obedience. "The oracle needs space." Then, to her, he whispered, "At ease, my lady, they mean you no harm. They only wish to welcome you."

Paige relaxed by small degrees, but still kept a wary eye on the crowd. Aidan didn't let go of her waist and she squirmed, uncomfortable with the public claim. Every part of her wanted to run away into the trees and hide. What was she doing here? In a town filled with strangers who would undoubtedly blame her when her prediction came true and a life was lost.

When Paige didn't speak to the expectant onlookers, Aidan cleared his throat. "Lady Paige has foreseen a terrible storm on the water tonight. All fishermen should be called in."

"And lose a day of work while the blugin run?" a man with short black hair yelled. "We only have two nights to pull the supplies we need to last a year. Who will feed our children when the food runs out next winter?"

"The rest of the season's catch won't compare to the blugin run," said a blonde woman with a small boy huddled into her skirts.

Paige looked at the young boy's face. Her voice soft and a little too high for normal, she said, "There is no reason you all have to stay ashore, so long as you come back when you feel the storm. We are only concerned about one man in particular. We're searching for a man with a scar."

"She doesn't act like the other oracles. Have her powers been tested?" someone asked.

"You expect us to stay out of the water on an untested prediction?" another added.

"Some prediction!" a woman cackled sarcastically. The tight pull of her laced bodice squeezed a pair of very generous breasts to the point they looked as if they might burst. "A man with a scar in Staria? If that's a prediction, I can do you one better. I predict I have five husbands."

A round of laughter instantly filled the center square.

"We are all oracles. I predict trees are growing in the forest," a voice mocked. "And those trees have leaves."

"I predict my wife will slap me," another man added, "for saying she's got a large—"

Sure enough, a woman slapped the man upside the head, stopping the rest of the comment.

"Is this the scar you are looking for, Lady Paige?" The black-haired man showed a red, puffy gash across his stomach before turning to let her see rounded marks on his back. "Or these?"

Instantly trying to outdo each other, the men

lifted their shirts and pulled at their sleeves, pointing out their many scars. Even the boys joined in the teasing.

"I have nigh twenty, my lady, if you count the ones run together," someone hollered.

"And I nigh thirty," another voice chimed.

"Forty here!"

"Forty-one!"

"I have one, my lady," a child yelled, shoving his stick under his arm to hold it in place as he struggled with his neckline.

Behind her she felt Aidan shake as if holding back his own laughter. In her ear he whispered, "They are only teasing. They must like you."

This was how they greeted people they liked? Paige didn't say a word.

"I have got a scar to show you, but it's on my arse." This response got a solid thump in the chest from the man's wife and more laughter from the crowd.

That was it! Prying at his arm, she got him to loosen his hold on her waist. Swinging her leg around the side, she slid from the horse. Her legs wobbled as they hit the ground. If they only wanted to mock her, then the lot of them could rot for all she cared.

"We're looking for an older man with a scar

across the back of his hand. Jagged," Aidan said. She heard him land on the ground behind her. Paige inched away from him, eyeing the crowd for her easiest escape. As the new woman wearing unsuitable attire, she knew it wouldn't be easy to blend. No, her best bet was slipping notice while Aidan was distracted. Then she would head for the trees.

"Do you speak of Callum?" someone offered. "He has such a scar."

"Aye, I have a scar on my hand."

Paige turned to find the man from her vision staring at her. Instantly, she sought his hand, finding the exact scar she had pictured. All thoughts left her as she whispered, "That scar. It's you. You're the man I saw."

Callum rubbed the back of his hand with his thumb, but the gruff lines of his weathered face didn't flinch. "A barbed hook caught it during blugin season when I was a boy. We had no choice but to rip it out and bandage it up." He flexed his hand.

"Don't go to the water tonight. Stay inside." Almost desperate, she rushed forward. Never had she been so close to saving a life before. The Forestters didn't want to hear about her visions, didn't want her help. They threatened and blamed her for whatever misfortune came if she tried. "If you take to the sea, you'll be killed when the waves destroy your boat. Try to stay away from all water, just to be safe."

Again, Callum didn't flinch. Worry didn't enter his steady gaze, but neither did doubt. He dropped his hand. Nodding once, he said, "Thank you for the warning, oracle."

Then, turning, he picked up a bucket of water from the ground and carried it down the road as if nothing in his life had changed. Paige lifted her hand, thinking to stop him. "But..."

"Rejoice, the oracle has spoken!" someone yelled causing her to jump in surprise. The cry was followed with shouts of, "Rejoice! Rejoice!"

Even Aidan uttered a very low, "Rejoice," while looking at her with his hot, seductive eyes. There was something else in his gaze—pride. She trembled, overwhelmed by the crowd's acceptance and excitement.

"Come on then, we have duties to attend to." A plump woman waved her hand, ushering a couple boys into one of the nearby shops. The crowd followed her lead and began to disperse. A few even paused to congratulate her on her marriage.

"But..." Paige jerked as Aidan touched her elbow.

"Are you hungry, my lady? The Axe Hitter Tavern will gladly take our coin."

"I don't have coin," Paige answered without thinking. She lifted her hand to point down the road Callum was quickly disappearing. "Did he not believe me? I'm not teasing him. I really did see his fate on the water."

"I'm sure he believes you. Had he not, Callum would have laughed at you and denounced your claim. See, all is well. He goes home. You have done what you've come to the village to do." This time he grabbed her arm and forcibly made her turn toward the horse. "Callum will make his decision."

Not wanting to sit close to him again and subject herself to another round of agonizingly unfulfilled desires, she shook her head. "I think I would rather walk."

"As you wish," he answered. His low voice sent an animalistic thrill over her.

Heat curled in her stomach and she realized she didn't have to sit next to him to feel the pain of hunger and need. Just knowing Aidan was near caused her body to respond with wet passion. Her throat dry, she managed to inquire, "Which way to the tavern?"

4

BY ALL THE bloody swords in Staria, Aidan wanted her like he'd never wanted anything in his life. Everything about her caused his blood to boil in his veins until he had to actively focus his thoughts to keep from fantasizing. He suppressed a groan. Everywhere he looked, he thought of ways to take her against him—behind cottages, against trees, over the table that now stood between them. It was madness and he wasn't sure he wanted to find a cure for it.

Aidan found it hard to swallow his meal as he watched Paige's tongue trail across her bottom lip to sweep a small bread crumb into her mouth. The tavern was empty, which wasn't unusual for that time of morning. Many would have had their morn meal before the sun rose over the earth.

Set along the edge of town, the Axe Hitter Tavern brewed most of the town's ale and became a natural gathering place for the locals. A sweet tinge of liquor always flavored the air, seeping into the main building from the stone structure around back.

Rough-hewn boards held together with plaster formed the tavern building walls. According to the owner, Merrit, the design came from her homeland. Inside, wooden tables and equally plain chairs lined up like soldiers in orderly rows. Strips of material, bright and festive like a lady's skirts, covered abnormally large windows. Because of the large oven, the room was warmer than outside, but a pleasant breeze through the opened door made it agreeable. Having Paige as his company made it even more so. Even if she didn't say much, the growing gleam in her eyes said more than words ever could.

"How is your mother, Sir Aidan?" Merrit asked him, sauntering to the table. Though tall and slender, there was a seedy coarseness to the inviting sway of her hips. Wherever the fairies had sent this woman from had been a hard place. She ran the Axe Hitter with her husbands.

"Still at sea," Aidan answered. "I don't imagine she will be back before midsummer."

"Still swimming away from the suitors is what

you mean to say," Merrit chuckled. "Hasn't Martin caught her yet?"

"No, not yet. Though I doubt she is worried. With you in town there are no men left without a bride. How many do you have now? Thirty-seven?"

"Eleven. Poor Tomm died last winter." Merrit clicked her tongue, lightly running her hand over her red curls. "It is a shame. He was a good man, if not a little bit of a stinker. I hated to lose one of my collection. I don't suppose you want to replace him? Come on, Sir Aidan, be the first Starian man to take two wives. We will change the world, the three of us."

To Aidan's pleasure, he saw Paige's fist tighten over her bread. She stopped eating but didn't interrupt Merrit's banter.

Aidan laughed at the very absurdity of the idea, thoughtlessly giving her a small grin. "I am not sure that would work or that it would have the gods' blessing, for to do so I would be taking on eleven husbands and you a wife. I will have to decline."

"I don't know about your gods, Sir Aidan, but mine heartily approve." Merrit swiped the two nearly empty trenchers of food from their table. "Help yourself to the rooms in back. They're not all clean but they are all empty." With a wink she left, leaving them with only themselves and a couple of goblets of slightly soured ale.

"You have a mother?" Paige asked, her eyes steadily on his face.

"Doesn't every man?" he chuckled, his mind instantly taking his gaze to the hall leading back to where Merrit put up travelers for the night.

"I meant alive. You have family?" She licked her bottom lip. By the teeth of the damned, did she have to keep doing that? His cock lurched in his pants, demanding the full focus of his brain.

"Ah," he took a drink, gulping down the liquor. When he could again think, he said, "My mother, Lady Carrina, is at sea."

Paige glanced at Merrit. "I heard."

"Yea, I suppose you did. My mother spends most of her life at sea these days. Ocean life agrees with her, or so she says. She was born here in Fallenrock Village to a fisherman."

"And this Martin?" she prompted.

"Martin wishes to claim my mother, but he cannot seem to catch her." Aidan shook his head, amused and a little sorry for the old warrior. "She left after my father died and only sneaks back at night in the middle of summer to avoid being claimed a second time."

"And is she an oracle too? Is that why you don't question what I say?"

"No. She is not, though I sometimes think she wishes she'd been so blessed. And why would I question you? You have no reason to deceive me." Aidan leaned closer, reaching out to touch her hand as it lay on the table. She pulled it just out of reach.

"Do you have brothers or sisters?"

"No sisters. My family was not blessed with girls." Aidan went on to explain the Starian's lack of daughters and need for wives. He wasn't sure why, but he felt himself rambling, anything to bring forth hints of interest to her green eyes. "I had brothers but they were killed in battle. And you?"

"Everyone I had is dead." Short. Simple. That was all the answer she would give him.

"Did your family possess gifts?" he asked.

"Just my grandmother and my father. I suppose I'll pass it to some of my children." She paused, not meeting his eyes at that last comment about children. Clearing her throat uncomfortably, she continued, "But the Forestters don't call them gifts."

"Ah, that's right. You said you were cursed." Aidan again reached to touch her, more quickly this time so she didn't have a chance to pull back. He held her small hand easily under his larger one, conscious of the delicate fingers curling against the tabletop. "I don't think I'd ever understand people who look at such a blessing as a curse. Without you, Callum would take to the sea, unknowing of his fate, unable to do what he must."

She visibly swallowed. "Do you really think I saved him?"

The need in her expression was tinged with fear. He wondered exactly how badly she had been treated by her people because of her "curse". Smiling, he held her hand tighter. "You did well, my lady. Do not worry yourself about Callum. You did what you could by him."

* * *

Paige's heart raced until she was sure it would explode. Inside the tavern, hidden in the dim light away from the crowd, she had begun to relax, but now Aidan's hand on hers made her all too aware of his touch. A nervous, excited tremble began at the contact and radiated up her arm and throughout her body. No man looked at her the way he did, hot and liquid and unafraid. His passion intrigued and frightened her. She was scared to want him as much as she did, scared of what it could mean, of what could be won and lost in his embrace. A small whisper in the back of her mind told her to run away until she could reason out what was happening, but that whisper was drowned out by the thumping of her heartbeat echoing in her ears.

Out of all the times she had tried, she had never been able to save a life before. Her grandmother had spoken of it several times, of how some man in their family lineage had kept his entire planet from being destroyed. Though, Paige's visions were nowhere near as powerful as those. Her sight was tied to the weather. She saw death by water or air or earth, but never by a human hand. Her grandmother always told her to be patient, that more visions would come. Paige didn't want them to get stronger.

"Tell me about you, my lady. You have listened to me talk, but you have said little about your life beyond short, necessary answers." He looked so sincere, so eager to know her. "I would know more."

Paige opened her mouth, but an answer didn't readily come. Living alone for the last several years had only taught her to talk to herself and the trees. "I hate crowds."

"I gathered as much," he chuckled. "You looked as if you couldn't run away fast enough. What else do you hate?"

I hate seeing visions of people dying. I hate being treated like an outsider. I hate that fear people get in their eyes when they get too close to me. I hate the Faerians, but perhaps just a little less than I did this morning. I hate the way you're looking at me now, like you know a secret that I should know too. And I hate Merrit for disregarding me while she tried to make you a twelfth husband—even though that doesn't mean I want you for my husband. Because I don't.

Paige frowned. Was it possible that her brain actually started laughing at her?

"This ale tastes off. I don't like it very much," she whispered so Merrit couldn't hear her. Paige touched the rim of the goblet.

"It is a little past its time," he agreed. "What else don't you like?"

She gestured helplessly, trying to pull her hand from his. The warmth tingled up her arm and she took a deep breath as she stared at his larger palm engulfing hers.

"Then, what do you like?" His fingers moved. She couldn't see it, but she could feel it, a tiny vibration along her flesh.

"Rain," she said simply. "When it falls all around me, my head is quiet. It washes my thoughts and I don't have to see anything. Sometimes I wish it always rained."

"Then I was right, you are where you belong. It rains almost nightly in Fallenrock." This time she did see his finger move. His thumb brushed along her wrist, as if strumming an invisible thread from her hand to her chest. A second hand captured her free one, pressing it to the tabletop. Her heart pounded, beating a rhythm in her ears.

"I like music and hearing people sing. Sometimes I would sneak to the edge of the village and listen to the festivals from the trees. Music always sounds better over a distance. I always wished there was a way to capture the music and replay it back later. Silly, huh? Like we'd ever be able to capture something as fleeting as sound." Paige sighed, closing her eyes slightly. Her limbs felt heavy and energetic at the same time. Her breasts ached and she clamped her legs together to keep the sensation from spreading downward. It didn't work. Her sex dampened with desire.

"What else?" he whispered, the sound a little hoarse.

The room appeared to blur as she looked at his face. Had he leaned closer? "I like, ah..." Paige let loose a shaky breath.

I like your forest-colored eyes? I like your slightly crooked smile? I like you, your...

"I like your fire boxes." If he wasn't holding her hands down she would have smacked herself across the cheek.

Fire boxes?!

"Fire boxes?" He turned, his hands slipping somewhat as he looked at the wall. "You mean the fireplace?"

Paige nodded.

"You don't have..."

"Our place for fire is in pits in the center of a home." Was she a complete imbecile? What was she even talking about? And why couldn't she concentrate?

"I like your soft skin." His fingers massaged deeper into her flesh. "Your deep, green eyes so full of mysteries I can't wait to unravel. Your red hair that—"

"Aidan," she tried to stop him. "You're..."

"I'm?" There was that crooked smile again—utterly charming and completely devastating.

"I'm," she started a second time, struggling with the words.

"You're?" How did he get so close, leaning into

her from across the table? When she didn't find the words, he stood, pulling her with him.

Paige couldn't think of what to do, so she followed him, letting him lead her through the main room of the tavern toward a back hallway. The faint sound of Merrit's laughter penetrated the fog in her brain but it wasn't enough to draw her out of the trance Aidan placed over her senses.

Wood walls striped with white passed along either side of them. Aidan led her to the back before opening a door and pulling her inside. She got the briefest glimpse of a trunk and bed before Aidan jerked her into his chest. Fiery heat exploded where he touched, spreading throughout her with a mind-swirling speed. She gasped and he drew his lips down to devour hers.

What is happening to me?

Aidan's tongue slid over her mouth, translating the desperation of his body. Before she could react, he turned, pressing her back into the rough-hewn wall. The unmistakable outline of his arousal dug into her stomach. She had felt hints of it as they rode but had forced herself to ignore it. Now, with the evidence of his desire so blatant, she couldn't think of anything else.

"Such softness beneath these clothes," he

groaned into her mouth as a hand cupped her breast through the shirt she had taken from his trunk.

Such hardness beneath yours, she thought.

Tentatively, she touched his arms, sliding her fingers down his biceps to his elbows, only to let them drop to his waist and continue along his thighs. The hilt of the knife bumped her hand and she thought about taking it. Paige hesitated too long because Aidan grabbed it first, broke the kiss and turned to throw it at the wall. It stuck into the wood plank above the bed, vibrating before coming to rest.

His actions became more aggressive. He delved his hand beneath her shirt, instantly grabbing a naked breast. His hips ground into hers, forcing her ass hard against the wall. Paige turned her head before he could kiss her, gasping for air. He didn't stop. His lips found her neck only to bite and lick a trail along her jaw to her earlobe. Heavy breath surrounded her, cocooning her inside the rapid sensations.

"Aidan," she panted, fighting in a sea of desire and fear. Her body ached for him, but already he reached between them to free his cock from his breeches. "Aidan, no."

He groaned into her neck, a sound of pain and frustration. When she expected him to yell or ignore her, he asked, "Do you still hurt? Was this morning too soon?"

"It's not that. I..." She swallowed nervously, her fingers digging into his upper arms. "I don't..."

"You don't want this?" The sound in his voice tore at her, but he didn't back away.

"I don't know what I'm doing."

That brought him back. "But, before—"

"Fairy magic. They poisoned me. I haven't..." She couldn't look at his eyes. They were too penetrating. She felt a slight flush heating her cheeks with embarrassment. "Men in my village are afraid of me. After I told them of the earth opening up and they didn't listen, they blamed me for causing the deaths with my curse since I'd spoken the words out loud. I was eleven when it happened and every man has been too afraid to come near me."

Not that I wanted them near me. Not like this.

"So I haven't, I mean I don't know... I'm really bad at this." Paige let go of him to fan her face. Every nerve in her body had been brought to stinging life. "I think I need air."

"Methinks you need a husband who is gentler." He cupped her cheek and turned her jaw so she looked at him. "Forgive me. It is not in a warrior's nature to be tender, but I see the fear in your eyes when you look at me now and I do not like it. I will try harder to please you."

When he moved away, she expected him to lead her back out into the main part of the tavern. Instead, he pulled her toward the bed. When he let go of her, he tugged at his tunic shirt and tossed it aside. He eyed her expectantly, as if waiting for her to do the same.

Without the same grace of movement he displayed, she obeyed the silent command. She pulled the shirt over her head and let it drop on the floor by her feet. Paige watched his face, not moving to cover herself.

Aidan drew his finger over her stomach, tracing the long scar from her navel to beneath her armpit. "Any warrior would be proud to wear this."

Proud? She should be proud about being flayed alive?

"To survive such a wound shows you have strength. I would happily show it to the others, but I don't think I want them looking at you so intimately." He traced it back down and up again, the finger an odd contrast to her cooling skin. "How did you receive it?"

"Some of the children were not happy when their parents were swallowed by the ground," she answered. Paige could still see their childhood faces, contorted with hate and nightmares. "They came for me convinced if they killed me they could trade my life for their parents'. My father stopped them, but was almost too late."

Aidan sank to his knees slowly. He leaned over, brushing his lips against her flesh. He traced the scar with light, feathery kisses before his knees finally reached the floor. He knelt before her, his hands on her waist. Tugging at the laces along her hips, he loosened her waistband.

"You do not have to worry about such things anymore. Here you will be protected. I will let no harm come to you," he said.

"What about when you leave for war?" She touched the top of his head, running her hand over the silken texture of his blond hair.

"Should there be an attack this far north you'd be taken to the castle with the other oracles. Every man in Fallenrock would die protecting you." The laces at her waist loosened and he tugged at her pant legs. He kissed her exposed hip.

"I don't want that, Aidan." She pulled his hair, turning his face away from her stomach to look at her. "I can take care of myself. I've been doing it for a long time now. Please understand I don't want people dying for me."

"But you're a woman." Aidan's hands splayed over her hips, bringing her body closer so he could rub his cheek against her. The subtle hint of whiskers scratched her, but the sensation was hardly unpleasant. "Women are to be protected and cared for. What better cause to fight for than in protection of the fairer sex?"

The way he said it—simple, factual, indisputable —made her tremble.

"You are my wife. I would be a disgrace as a soldier if I did not lay down my life for you." His hands slid down her hips, pushing the pants down to spill around her ankles. He squeezed her ass, drawing her body closer still as he turned his mouth to brush over the soft red curls. Her legs shook, instantly weak as warm breath fanned across her sex.

If what he was doing didn't feel so good, she would have run from the room to calm the emotions running rampant inside of her. "Aidan, you don't know me."

"I know the gods sent you to me. I asked them for a bride and they gave me you." A low moan escaped him and he became more aggressive with his kisses— biting and licking a hot trail over her lower stomach and thighs. The little nips teased her, making her hot for a more intimate contact.

Paige never held out much realistic hope that she would someday find a husband, but in her unspoken fantasies she was like any woman. Who didn't want a man strong enough to protect his woman? But she didn't just want a man who'd die fighting for her. She wanted a man who loved her, adored her and needed to be near her. Aidan offered half of the fantasy. Could she really complain if he didn't offer it all? It's not like she had men lining up at her door in her realm. Wasn't something better than nothing? She wouldn't have to be alone the rest of her life, and when he went off to war she would be left to live in the forest just as she liked.

Unsure if she had actually come to a decision, Paige closed her eyes and let the sensations of his kiss wash over her. He massaged her ass and the backs of her thighs, only to caress up her lower back and down her legs. She had never been touched so completely before and her flesh was starved for the contact. Her fingers slipped from his head to rest on his shoulders for support.

Aidan reached for her breasts, but when he moved his hands from behind her, she stumbled back and bumped into the bed, immediately falling to sit on the stiff mattress. He walked on his knees, coming to her. With a firm shove, he spread her thighs. Paige stared at him, wide-eyed as he lowered his face between her legs. A loud moan sounded seconds before his mouth captured her clit in a deep kiss. His tongue lapped up her slick folds, kissing and sucking and tasting.

She gasped, falling back with the intention of lying on the bed. Her head bumped into the wall and she jerked. "Ow!"

Aidan chuckled, lifting his head from her. "Turn."

Paige wrinkled her nose at his amusement, rubbing her sore scalp, even as she obeyed. Stretching out on the mattress, she forgot all about her injury as Aidan crawled on top of her.

"It is taking every ounce of my control not to wildly take you as we did in the forest." He nuzzled her neck while palming a breast. "But if I have to be tortured, I would have it at your hand, my lady."

"This is madness," Paige whispered as she touched his cheek. He didn't answer but to bite at her earlobe.

Aidan reached between them and she felt his hand working at his laces, bumping along her pussy and thighs. The clarity of the moment was a stark contrast to the times before. Her brain registered every little detail and captured it. She moved restlessly beneath him, her entire being growing hotter with each passing moment.

Aidan's hot breath fanned her neck with warmth. His chest teased her hardened nipples, tickling them as she moved. The back of his hand stroked her sex, sending a delicious sensation over her clit. Paige couldn't help herself. She arched her hips so they again rubbed against each other. A light moan of pleasure escaped her and she closed her eyes.

When Aidan freed himself from his pants, he removed his hand and braced his weight on the bed. Lifting up, he untangled his legs and fitted them between hers, holding her open. Their bodies moved restlessly against each other. The stiff bed pressed into her back, but she didn't notice it. How could she when he looked at her the way he was? His lids fell over his eyes, shading them as he studied her face. They moved over her, as if memorizing every detail. Had she been standing, she would have run from his deep perusal—not because she didn't like it, but because the intensity frightened her.

The strands of his hair framed his face as he maneuvered his hips. The first brush of his cock along the wet folds of her sex made her jolt involuntarily. She remembered what it felt like, his thick body pushing roughly into hers, stretching, pounding, claiming.

But instead of the hard thrust, he took her gently, easing his way in with a controlled push of his hips. Aidan bit his lip, sighing even as he tensed. The thick splay of muscles across his chest moved erotically beneath the skin. Paige held onto his arms as her body accepted him.

The intensity of his eyes burned into her, capturing her until she couldn't look away. Aidan took his time, slowly pulling out and thrusting in a seamless, perfect motion. His scent surrounded her, fresh and clean yet tinged with the herbs of the forest.

Paige worked her legs against the bed, digging her heels into the mattress. Her hands glided restlessly over his body, touching everywhere she could reach. Leaning slightly to the side, he grabbed her thigh, lifting it high along his hip while he continued to thrust. The new position brought him deeper and her entire being shuddered in response.

She moaned, suddenly clawing at his firm ass. The pleasure built into a frenzied tension. She couldn't catch her breath, couldn't stop moving her hips. Aidan grunted, his movements becoming harder as he quickened his pace. He grabbed her breast, massaging it briefly before again bracing his weight on the bed.

"Ah," he groaned. "By all the sword blades in Staria, you feel like a fresh victory."

Paige didn't know how to respond to the strange compliment so she moaned incoherently instead. Tremors took hold of her stomach, shaking their way from her sex to the rest of her body. She tensed only to jerk several times as she met with release. Aidan looked down at her like a man who'd just conquered his world, joining her with his own heavy climax.

5

Rain pelted her face and chest, but Paige made no move to get out of the foul weather. Even cold and hard, the droplets felt as close to heaven as she had ever been. Each one hit her flesh like a tiny blade, sharp and poignant, leaving behind a shard of numbness that slowly spread over her limbs.

With little effort, her head cleared until no thoughts flowed but her own. She breathed deeply, loving the absence of emotions. Normally her body felt like a breeding ground for strange feelings, but now, in the rain, she felt only herself. It was only in these moments she had any kind of real clarity.

What in the green of the forest am I doing here?

After the rush of sexual release in the tavern— and again in the forest on the way back to Aidan's home, and pressed up against the stables after stalling the horse, oh, and lest she forget the side of the house because they didn't make it inside after the stables—she had felt the call of the oncoming rain.

The storm from her vision started with a few gentle drops snaking down Aidan's strong face as the magenta light of evening darkened his features. Hope and excitement warred with the fear of disappointment. She couldn't keep kissing Aidan, exploring his touches and his embrace, with the reminder that a life might end on the sea. When Aidan led her inside with the offer of sleep and food, she had followed only to slip away the second his attention turned from her to slice strips of meat on a cutting table.

What do I do? Stay? Go? This is not my homeland.

Paige turned to look at the looming house cast in blue moonlight.

This is not my home.

"But it could be," she whispered.

The cold water stuck the borrowed tunic to her flesh and the wind blew it tight to her chest. Strands of her hair plastered against her neck and cheeks. She didn't bother to pull them off.

"I could live here," she continued, "as an oracle. I could save lives."

Did she dare to hope?

The frigid water combined with the rush of chilly air coming off the sea became almost unbearable, but she was hesitant to leave the clarity of the rain. Inside, she would have to work to keep the visions from rushing back in—not as hard as when the skies were clear, but she would have to work all the same—and she still didn't know what she wanted to do about Aidan. She did not share his confidence in their joined futures.

Paige turned into the trees. Now that was a life she did understand—uncomplicated, peaceful, free. The building smile faded before it had a chance to grow. And that life was very, very lonely.

Hands wrapped her waist from behind, drawing a startled gasp from her. Aidan's voice rose above the pounding rhythm of the raindrops hitting the earth. "I understand your need for silence, but I worry about you in this weather. The cold sea rain can cause a breathing sickness."

Even after the day they'd spent having sex, she still felt the quivering temptation of his touch. The heat of his body chased away the chilly rain and Paige found she didn't mind the jumbling of her thoughts as her focus turned from the weather to Aidan's strength. When he hugged her tighter, she dropped her head back against his chest. Aidan's chin moved down along her ear, coming to rest near her cheek as he curled around her. The now very familiar rub of his growing erection brushed along her ass.

"Come inside." Aidan gently pulled her with him a couple steps before sweeping her up into his arms. Cradling her against his body, he hurried to the opened door of his house. He kissed the corner of her mouth before dropping her legs to set her down on the floor. "If you desire a bath to warm yourself, the bathing room is at the end of the hallway. Lift and push the pump handle and the water will flow. I will finish cooking."

"You have bathing water in the house?" Curious, she turned from him. Water dripped from her clothes and the smell of cooking food followed her as she made her way down the hall. Pushing open the door, she found a large, smooth stone hole in the floor. Lidded jars lined the far edge and a hand pump rose from the ground. Though the design differed from what she was used to seeing, she could determine its function easily enough.

As she lifted and pumped the handle, a stream of dark blue water poured from the spigot into the bathing pool. Paige watched, mesmerized, and lifted her hand to watch the gemlike water trail over her skin in sparkling rivulets. Why hadn't the Forestters thought of indoor water pumps? They had to cart water from the outside brooks to a giant storage bin.

Standing, she peeled off her wet clothes. Warm water tickled her legs, lapping gently as she moved into the bathing pool. Sinking into the depths, she perched her ass on the edge of an underwater seat and sighed with relief as heat enveloped her. Tension eased out of her shoulders and neck, causing a tingling sensation on her scalp.

Paige rubbed her shoulder, liking the way her fingers slipped over flesh with aid of the water. Watching the door for signs of movement, she wondered if Aidan would follow. When he didn't she moved her hands to her breasts, massaging them gently. In light of the pleasure Aidan had shown her, her sensitive body was only too willing to find release again.

Paige ran her hand down her stomach, tracing the scar that led to her parted thighs. The warm bath made her sex so wet and hot and rubbing along the slit was both easy and highly pleasurable. She kept her eyes on the door, not wanting him to catch her as she slipped a finger inside. Wiggling the digit in small circles, she tried to mimic his touch. She clamped her thighs tight against her hand, holding it in place. Her hips rocked so that her clit brushed up against her palm.

She suppressed a moan. The heated water lapped against the top of her breasts and neck, the surface rippling with her movements. Her lids fell heavy over her eyes, but she didn't look away from the door. Thoughts of Aidan swam in her brain. Paige panted, biting her lip hard as her hand worked harder and faster. She grabbed a breast, pinching the nipple between two fingers. Never had self-pleasure felt so good.

Her body tensed as small tremors started in her pussy and traveled out over her entire length. Breathing heavily, Paige closed her eyes, letting the relaxation settle into her muscles. Her legs fell limp to release her hand.

"Aidan," she whispered, awash in pleasure.

AIDAN LOOKED DOWN at the trencher of food he had prepared for his new bride. Strips of meat piled in the center surrounded by the last of his vegetables. With the house left empty most of the time, there'd been little need to see to the planting and storage. He had let the villagers who took care of his home use the garden space. When he had been a boy the larder had been overflowing with food and the house always smelled of his mother's cooking.

"Soon we will fill this house with a family," he said to himself. "Now is the time for patience. I have had more of her than any man could ask. It was wise of the ancestors to assign women separate bedchambers." The reasonable sound of his own voice did not ease the ache in his loins. He wanted nothing more than to grab her, hold her close and spend the rest of his time at home in her arms.

Carrying the tray in one hand and a jug of ale in the other, he began walking toward the bathing room only to hesitate. They had been together all day. Was it too much? She had gone outside to be alone and he had interrupted her. No matter how eager he was to see her naked in his bath, he wondered if he shouldn't give her some time alone.

Thinking of the warm blue water clinging to her delectable nipples caused him to bite his lip and moan. He started for the bathing room door. Then, remembering how she had looked out in the rain, her face turned to the sky with a look of complete and open rapture when she didn't know he watched her, he stopped and went back to the dining table.

"Ach! What are you doing, boy? Leaving my door open to invite the storm in?"

Aidan turned, pushing up from the table before he had a chance to sit down. A smile broke across his face at the voice. "Mother. You're back."

"Just this eve. The gods are angry tonight. They finally chased me off the sea," Carrina of Fallenrock answered her son. Lines of age had been smoothed by the salt of the open sea air. A rasp resounded in her voice, a sound that had not been there when he was younger.

Aidan gave her a hug, affectionately patting her short gray hair. "And I imagine Martin will chase you back onto the waves come sunup."

"It's safer ashore while the blugin run the next couple of days." She chuckled. Time and loss had taken their toll and he saw that toll in her serious eyes. Even when she laughed the sadness was there. Unlike most women of Staria, she wore the white tunic and breeches of a sailor. The clothes had been yellowed by years on the sea and worn to the point no one would suspect her to be a woman from such a prestigious family. Aidan was pretty sure that was why she looked the way she did. The disguise hid her identity and, if she mentioned having a "husband" or two, very few men would try to claim her without first seeking permission from her nonexistent spouses. "Ah, food."

Aidan glanced toward the bathing room. Paige was too far away to hear them.

As Carrina reached for the tray of cooked meat, she continued, "I skirted the edge of town on my way here. There's talk of a new oracle in the area. It was a little hard to make out everything, but I hear she is beautiful and has come through the fairy rings." Taking a bite, she grinned meaningfully at him. "As the highest-ranking man in the village and a sacred protector of the oracles, you should lay claim to her before any others."

"Here two seconds and you're already scheming to see me wed. Hm, should I return the favor? Martin would be very pleased to receive a missive as to your joyous return and unclaimed status. I am sure the whole village would rejoice in celebration."

Carrina grabbed another meat strip and gestured it toward him with a suppressed laugh. "And that would make him the master of this house and your new father."

"Point taken." Aidan grabbed a strip and bit into it.

"Aidan, my clothes are wet and I didn't see anything to dry off with." Paige emerged from the hall, dripping with water and wearing nothing but an arm across her chest and a hand splayed over her sex to mimic clothing. "Do you have—oh, blessed forest!" Paige's loud scream and pounding footfall were only outdone by Carrina's shout of surprised laughter.

A door slammed, encouraging Aidan to go after his bride. To his mother he said, "The oracle has already been claimed."

Carrina's squeal of delight followed him down the hall.

Tracking the wet footsteps to the room he had laid Paige in when he first brought her home, he pushed open the door without knocking. He couldn't help the smile that curled on his lips to see her naked ass pointing in his direction as she dug through the trunk of clothing. She gasped, twirling around with a tunic pressed to her chest to hide her wet body.

"I'm taking the food to my room!" his mother yelled through the door. "I want grandchildren!"

Paige flinched. Aidan tried to give her what he hoped was an apologetic look. "That's my mother. Apparently, your storm chased her from the sea."

"It's not my storm." Paige stiffened. "I didn't make it rain. I told you already. I can't control the weather or what it does to—"

"Paige, calm yourself. I did not mean to imply you had aught to do with—"

"Calm myself? Calm myself!" She gave a wry laugh. Then to herself, she mumbled, "What am I doing here?"

Aidan hated to see the look on her face, lost and perhaps a bit frightened. He had expected modesty and embarrassment, but not that.

"It has been a long day for you." He resisted the urge to go to her. He was a warrior and wasn't sure what to say to comfort her. Yelling at her as he would a fresh knight scared of the battlefield hardly seemed appropriate. "I will leave you to rest. Please, let me know if you have needs."

She didn't answer, only continued to stare at him with her wide, confused eyes. Aidan slowly backed away, leaving her alone in the room.

"THIS IS MUCH MORE appropriate for a woman of your position. I cannot believe my son let you run around the village in his old clothes." Carrina nodded her head in approval, studying the gown she had forced Paige to wear. Well, "forced" might be a little harsh. It's not as if the woman pinned her down and held a knife to her throat. Instead, Carrina had used something even more fear-provoking—her determined stare, a stare that started the moment Paige opened her eyes to see the woman leaning over her.

Paige eyed the woman in return, taking in her yellowed, ill-fitted clothing. "A woman of my position?"

"As Lady Paige of Fallenrock, wife to Sir Aidan," the woman answered, as if it shouldn't have needed clarification.

Paige turned from the woman to look down at herself. Diffused, morning light shone through the narrow window, shadowed by falling rain. It created a strange streaking light across her exposed cleavage. The light green undertunic gown flowed around her hips and legs only to be pressed tight against her waist by the darker green corset. The tight bodice of the corset covered her bared nipples, but did little to hide the fact that her breasts had been pushed together and up like some sort of trophy display. The wide neckline exposed her shoulders and fell loose upon her upper arms before forming long, flowing sleeves. Reaching into the top of her bodice, she tried to fish the undertunic's neckline up and out to cover her chest. It was no use. There wasn't enough material.

"Ah, I knew this gown would fit you. Just don't let the townsfolk see it. I got it off Lixie's clean laundry pile last night." Carrina chuckled. "I have a bit of amusing gossip for you, Paige."

Paige didn't answer, only half listening as she tugged the laces binding her waist tight.

Carrina, completely oblivious to her companion's mood, continued, "Lixie wanted one of my sons for herself, but Aidan and his brothers were always off to war. Before she had a chance to work her wiles on them, her own first husband claimed her. Now you wear one of her best gowns. Though I doubt Lixie would find much amusement in the fact that her gown succeeded where she had not."

Paige had "borrowed" plenty of items when living on her own and didn't so much as blink at wearing the stolen gown. What did bother her was the lack of movement the gown allowed and the fact she could barely breathe with the corset pulled so tight. How could she make a run to the forest if she needed to get away?

"The larder is empty so Aidan is hunting this morning. He should have gone before the rains started, but then I suppose he has been preoccupied." Carrina gave another small laugh, seeming to entertain herself more than anything.

"Are you sure you're his mother?" Paige asked before she could stop herself. She wasn't used to mothers speaking so freely about their sons. All was known, but her people never spoke of such things in full detail.

Carrina laughed harder, the gruff sound booming in the room. "I suspect the sea might have swallowed my manners. It's been awhile since I have talked to people who are really there."

Paige turned, really looking into the woman's eyes for the first time. She saw Carrina's gaze shift, moving from Paige's face and gown to the fire box only to land on the narrow window. Paige understood that look, had felt it herself during those long, cold, isolated winters in the forest.

"I understand," Paige said. "I have heard the invisible conversations too. I believe the mind creates the insane to keep us sane. It will pass."

Carrina's inner wildness calmed and she nodded once. "This house is too quiet. You should have heard the sounds it made when all my boys were home. Now the walls echo silence. You must get pregnant and fill it with noise. I had six sons, you should have more. Eleven, no twelve, methinks, or a lucky thirteen. We could build more rooms at the end of the house, and with so many children it will be easy to replant the garden."

Paige tried to smile politely, but the urge to run filled her. Perhaps Carrina's sanity wasn't rooted in mild insanity. Perhaps she had really just gone mad alone on the sea. Perhaps losing five sons and a husband to war had done it.

"Aidan takes family very seriously and will agree, so it is settled. Thirteen children." Carrina grinned, spinning around the room. "And we shall name the first for my husband and five for Aidan's brothers." Hitting the wall, she stopped and placed her cheek to the stone. "This house will sing again." She petted the wall, as if it were a living thing. "Won't you, house, you will sing. Won't you whisper to me now? What do you think of our plan?"

Paige didn't move. Carrina blocked the only exit. Thinking to change the subject, she said, "If you have a bow, I can hunt."

Carrina blinked in surprise, as if coming out of a stupor. "You are a woman. You are to be protected and provided for. Did they not tell you your role?"

"Just because I'm a woman doesn't mean I need to be protected," Paige argued. "I have lived on my own for a very long time."

"There are rules," Carrina insisted. "Rules and ways and traditions."

"They are not my ways. I don't need to be taken care of. I don't even know if I want a husband and children." Why was she arguing with Aidan's mother? All Paige knew was that she would not be giving birth to thirteen boys—no matter how much this woman wanted her to.

"The gods chose you for my son," Carrina snapped. "You are his reward for bravery in battle. It is your duty to be a wife, to give him children and to keep his home. If you fail and my son dies in battle because you do not see to his needs, then his blood will be on your hands and I will make sure everyone knows it."

AIDAN'S BODY ached with the haul of a successful hunt and the chill of the wet, unpleasant day. Still, he couldn't help but smile as he saw his wife waiting for him in the doorway. It didn't matter what she wore— the belt of the fairies, his old tunic, nothing at all— she always looked beautiful to him. But to see her in the gown of his people, to see her as a true Starian woman should appear, caused his stomach to tighten with pleasure.

He would be blind to miss the way her breasts thrust up along the bodice, or the way the skirt clung to the curves of her hips to tease his senses. The length of her hair had been brushed back and bound at the nape of her slender neck. A few wisps of red had come loose and fell about her shoulders.

"Your mother left," she stated. "Something about spying on the town to make sure it's safe."

"A favorite pastime of hers, though I do not think it's the town's safety she is after as much as the town's gossip." He stopped near her, aware of what he must look like after a day of crawling around in the mud. Rain hit his back, the droplets not quite making it to where she stood beyond the stone doorstep. Shrugging a crossbow from his shoulder, he caught the strap with his hand. "What she won't tell you is that she is ultimately spying on Martin. Every time she comes back she leaves him a little hint that she was here. I'd almost feel sorry for the poor man, but since he can no longer fight in battle, I suspect it's her teasing that keeps him going. Even an old warrior enjoys the fight and intrigue."

He couldn't resist touching her and lifted his free hand to loop a finger around the soft red strands stirring closer to her face. Her lips parted ever so slightly and he imagined he could feel her breath against his wrist. A fine shiver worked over him, causing strange sensations to course through him. Ignoring the sudden rush of feeling, he turned his attention to where they touched and noticed the dirt marring his fingers as it contrasted her clean hair and face.

"I regret that you were embarrassed last night," Aidan said softly, loath to let her go. Every time he looked at her, he wanted to pull her close and kiss her. "I did not know we were to have a visitor."

"This gown is stolen." Paige gave a nervous laugh and looked down. Aidan followed her gaze, his attention stopping at her breasts. He licked his lips, wondering if she would protest being pulled out into the sprinkling rain so he could hold her.

"I should have provided gowns for you. We'll go to the village tomorrow to see the seamstress. You can have as many as you like." His eyes met hers and an intensity passed between them.

"You should come out of the rain." Paige took his hand, leading him into the house. Once inside, she let go and shut the door.

6

PAIGE TOOK AIDAN'S HAND, leading him down the hall toward the bathing room. She had thought of running when Carrina left her alone, but her legs wouldn't seem to move and she found herself waiting for him in the uncomfortable Starian gown. He had said he had family, but five dead brothers, a lost father and a mother whose brains had abandoned her? Paige's heart broke a little at the thought. No wonder he seemed overeager to have a wife. He was lonely.

When she opened the bathing room door, she wasn't sure what to say to him. So, instead, she went to the hand pump and began filling the bath with water. Finishing, she knelt by the edge, dipped her hand just below the surface and observed, "Water is clear in my homeland and we don't have it running indoors."

"From what I understand, it's clear in most planes. Here it's only the underground, blue mineral springs that flow this color. It stays warm no matter how long it is away from a heat source. There have been many winters that the springs have saved us from a cold death." Aidan placed his bow on the floor and untied his sword scabbard. After placing his sword by the bow, he added two knifes to the pile. "Aboveground, our water flows clear, or mostly clear."

With the tight bodice pushing into her stomach, Paige shifted her position to sit next to the water. She dipped her fingertips, lifting them so they rained sapphires. "Can you drink it?"

"Only if the circumstances are dire and you will die without. Too much will make you sick, but will keep you from dying of thirst."

She kept her eyes on the water, but from the corner of her vision she saw him pulling his tunic over his head. The sound of material dropping against stone caused her to stiffen. Paige dipped her hand again, watching the blue tint her long sleeve as it got too close to the surface. A warm hand skimmed the back of her neck and she turned to find Aidan's naked arousal before her. She looked up the length of his body, meeting his gaze.

"You are worth fighting an eternity of battles for, my oracle," he whispered, so soft she barely heard him. "And yet, when I look at you, I do not think of wars."

Paige tried to answer, but no one had ever said such a thing to her and she wasn't sure how to answer. Aidan stepped past her, into the water. She followed him with her eyes, watching the strong, flexing muscles of his ass as he moved. Blue water swallowed him into its depths, until even his head disappeared under the rippling surface.

When he reappeared, he leaned along the edge and sighed. "What is it you think when you look at me?"

"I think that you, ah..." Paige's hand shook as she skated her fingers along the surface, imagining them like two tiny legs on a wintery pond. She bit her bottom lip, saying thoughtfully, "I think you carry yourself like a warrior and I think you have a lot of scars."

He grinned, pleased with the compliment. Paige tried not to laugh.

"What else?" Aidan prompted, reaching for soap. Instead of going deeper, Paige flicked water at him. "You look like you've been crawling around in mud."

Aidan roughly rubbed his hands over his face, cleaning it before surging across the bath to reach her. Wet hands gripped her hips. "It is my honor to provide for you. I would not have you starve when I am away. I have asked some of the women from the village to help you plant the garden. It should be a good year for crops for a large portion of the land has been resting."

"I can feed myself," she assured him. "There is no need for them to come."

"It helps the villagers to have a joint garden. They'll get extra vegetables for their families and a portion will be sent to the soldiers." His hands tightened and his voice lowered. "Take down your hair."

Not waiting for her to obey, he pushed up from the bath and tugged at the pins holding her hair, taking his time as he found all of them. Finally free, the locks spilled over her shoulders. Paige ran her hands over her head, detecting how his fingers had wet strands of her hair. She pulled the bulk of it off her shoulder, moving it aside to allow him access.

Aidan nuzzled her neck from behind, moaning softly into her skin. The warmth of his breath fanned over her, causing her to shiver. Heat radiated off him, his flesh warmed by the blue water. She closed her eyes, feeling his hands on her stomach, working to free her from the tight hold of the corset. As the laces loosened, she breathed a deep sigh of relief.

Aidan's lips brushed along her shoulder, skimming so lightly she barely felt the touch. Her mind focused on him, the shifts of his body, the kiss of his breath, the sound of a water droplet hitting the surface of the bath when he moved. The bodice loosened more, allowing his roaming hands access beneath the stiff material. He skimmed the bottom curve of her breasts, but couldn't do much more with the bodice hampering his movements.

"Come into the bath," he whispered, pausing to nip at her earlobe. Paige trembled, lifting her arms to reach behind her head. She touched his hair, keeping his lips close to her neck. He kissed her hard, sucking and licking along her throat. Her heart beat fast, thumping uncontrollably in her chest.

Aidan broke the contact of his lips and tugged the corset over her lifted arms. He tossed it aside. The tunic dress's neckline slung low, baring her breasts and shoulders. Without the aid of the corset, the green material slid easy from her arms to pool around her waist.

Aidan's warmth encircled her once more and

Paige couldn't help but wonder if the fairies had known they were giving her such a man when they tossed her through the portal. Did the little creatures realize that a land such as Staria seemed like a paradise to a woman like her? Paige was a Forestter and this land was forest and earth and she understood it. Fallenrock's constant rain calmed her thoughts. Its people understood her curse and called it a blessing. Here she could do good deeds, save lives, have friends, be happy. For the first time in her life, she felt as if she could belong to a society, not cast out onto its edges.

Then there was Aidan, whose hands tried to protect and worship at the same time. He cupped her breasts, massaging gently with heated, wet hands. His lips resumed their kisses against her shoulder and throat. Slowly, he pulled her back. Her gown caught beneath her, tangling in her legs. Aidan caught her against him, slipping a hand under her ass to support her weight. With one gentle motion, he drew her into the bath completely, sinking into the water. Paige sat on his lap, her naked back pressed to his chest.

Aidan moaned, his hips arching beneath her, pressing his heavy cock along the cleft of her ass. The tips of her hair floated in the water around them, sticking to the sides of her breasts when she lifted up. Using the advantage of his position, Aidan explored her body. He pinched her nipples. Paige reached behind her, touching his hips briefly before gliding her hands over his. Bronzed tattooed flesh contrasted with her skin. His fingers worked beneath hers. Water lapped her skin, an erotic caress that enhanced the moment. She squirmed, restlessly working against his arousal, an arousal that grew larger with each press of her cheeks.

He hugged her tight, wrapping his arms around her to touch her stomach, hips, upper thighs and back to her breasts. Paige moaned, enjoying the firm sensation of his touch. With each passing second, his movements became more eager. The room faded away until all that existed was the thin space separating their bodies.

She needed him, needed his touch, needed to feel the strength of him inside her. Paige tried to lift up and angle her body, but Aidan stopped her. Instead, he reached between her thighs to torture the clit he found buried in the folds of her sex. Fire shot through her senses, centering over her breasts and pussy. Stroking her pussy with the full length of his hand, he kept her ass tight to his cock. Harsh breathing hit her neck as he rubbed himself against her. A finger slipped past her folds, pushing up into her wet sex only to wiggle back and forth.

Paige rode his hand, gasping at how good the position felt. Aidan bit at her shoulder, not hurting but definitely hard enough to let her know how he anguished for release.

"Argh," he groaned roughly, the sound impassioned and raw. His body jerked hard and she knew he spilled his seed into the water.

Paige let go, joining him in his pleasure. Tremors racked her, weakening her limbs. She collapsed against him, letting her head fall back onto his shoulder. He held her, his hand resting possessively on her breast.

"I did not mean to find release so fast," he admitted, "but you are too beautiful to resist."

Paige turned on his lap, straddling his legs to get more comfortable. The evidence of his desire had lessened somewhat, though his cock still remained partially lifted. Aidan looked deep into her eyes, as he pushed her hair back to better see her face. His intensity forced her to meet his gaze.

Within moments, the heat of his cock grew between them. Paige moaned, her pussy answering his primal call with a rush of moisture. She breathed deeply, holding onto his shoulders. The blunt tip of his erection drew along her sex, thick and hard. Paige impaled herself on him, unable to help the smile that spread over her features.

Aidan held her hips beneath the water, lifting her up only to let go so she slid onto his full length. His eyes stayed focused on her, silently commanding her to keep her eyes open. Paige held onto his neck, keeping a slow, deep rhythm. It felt too good to let the waves of release take her and she tried to hold back. But Aidan forced her up and down faster and harder. His breathing became a deep, harsh echo all around her. She tensed, unable to stave off the trembling rush of pleasure her climax wrought. His hands slid over her back.

"Ah," she panted weakly. His cry of passion answered her in a loud, conquering shout of release.

For a long, sweet moment she stayed on his lap, their bodies joined. She rested her forehead to his, still looking into his eyes, though her lids were heavy. When the pounding of her heart slowed, she lifted off his cock.

"The gods have truly rewarded me." He didn't look away. Even when she turned her gaze to the water, she could feel him studying her. "Together we will fill this house and..."

Paige stiffened, unable to keep the thought of thirteen children out of her head.

"What is it?" Aidan's eyes narrowed and the open expression on his face died a little beneath a hardened mask. She had been so caught up in his touch that she hadn't noticed the unusually affectionate look until it was gone.

"Can't we just be?" Paige bit her lip and tried to scoot off his lap. He held tight. "Can't we just make sure we're going to last before we start talking about children? There is no reason to rush into a union. We can just be..." She gestured helplessly, unable to think of the right words. "We can just be."

"Why would you deny we are joined? The gods have sent—"

"Your gods," she broke in.

"I don't understand. You said yourself the fairies sent you here. They do the bidding of my gods. I have acted as a man should act. I am a soldier, a knight, I have proven myself in battle. I have done my duty." He still didn't let go of her. If anything, his hands tightened on her hips, gripping so hard his fingers hurt her. "Why do you doubt my honor?"

"Ow, stop." She squirmed violently, trying to shake him off.

He instantly let go of her and drew his hands

back, appearing horrified at what he had done. "Paige, I did not mean to harm you."

She slipped off his lap into the depths of the water to hide her nakedness. With the sudden tension between them, she felt too exposed. "My desire to make sure we will last before making a big commitment has nothing to do with your honor and everything to do with prudence and good sense."

"I trust that you will be a good wife." He looked as if she had stabbed him in the chest. "You believe I will not uphold my end of the marriage. That is the only reason you would say such a thing to me. What is it? You do not think I will protect you? Feed you? Treat you well?"

"You can't trust me, Aidan, you don't know me." Why was this so hard to explain? Why couldn't he just let their relationship unfold with time? Why did it have to be marriage and children from the very first instant?

"I know you are an oracle, come to me from the Forestter people," he said. "I know that you are my blessing. Why would I question anything else? Why would I worry about things that have not happened, will not happen?"

"Yes, and I suppose you know I'm a woman and I have red hair," she answered wryly. "That is not who

I am. Those things are superficial. They do not matter."

"Then I will spend the years getting to know who you are." He clenched his hand into a tight fist and his features tightened on his face. "You are my wife."

"Are you telling me that there is never an unhappy marriage in Staria? That every claimed woman is happy and true to her husband?" Paige swiped her hair from her face, peeling the wet locks off her shoulders.

"Of course not, but I have faith that our marriage will be blessed. I have done everything I was supposed to do." He slammed his fist onto the edge of the bathing pool with a heavy thud. "Why are you making this complicated?"

"Why are you yelling at me?" She surged to her feet, not caring that she had begun screaming. "Because I don't want to have thirteen children? Because I'd like to learn a little bit more about the man who has claimed me? Because I want to learn more about this new world? You cannot fault me for that, Aidan."

"I will tell you what you need to know."

"Well, kiss my toes!" She snorted sarcastically, lifting her arms to the side in a wide, mocking gesture of relief. "Why didn't you say so? Had I known there was no need to think and decide for myself, I wouldn't have put up a fight. By all the trees, impregnate me, oh divine master. I am here to serve as the happy little house maiden."

"I do not like what you are saying. I never asked you to be—"

"Well, then maybe you should tell me what I need to say. However will I know what to do without your guidance, Sir Aidan?" The aftermath pleasure of their encounter drained from her limbs, replaced by anger. She needed to walk. She needed the forest. She needed out of his presence before she challenged him to battle.

"You misunderstood my meaning, my lady." Aidan stood, facing her. She couldn't help herself as her eyes dipped down over his spectacular form.

"I'm going for a walk." She pulled her tunic dress from the ground, not caring that it was damp in spots as she pulled it on her damp body. "Do not follow me."

"You are my bride, Paige," Aidan said in warning.

"So you keep saying," she grumbled. Slamming out of the bathing room, she marched down the hall, fighting the gown. Why wouldn't he just listen? Why couldn't he understand? Finally giving up, she tossed it aside and went to raid the trunk for the male clothing she had altered.

"Daughter!" Carrina called, her voice booming. The happy tone didn't last long. "What happened to your new gown? I told you to be careful with it. I only found you one."

"I'll be outside. So if you and your son wish to continue planning my life, I won't get in the way." She didn't stop as she met with the moonlight-tinted rain.

THE STORM REGAINED strength and raged for three days, barely lifting as the gods seemed to rain down some unknown vengeance upon the people of Fallen-rock. The foul weather kept Paige inside with Aidan and his mother. No amount of rooms could help her escape Carrina's scrutiny or Aidan's probing gaze. He looked as if he might speak, but held back, showing none of the affection he had before their argument.

Paige assumed the euphoria of her "marriage" to Aidan would have eventually faded, but after only one fight and a few days? It only proved her instinct was right. He pushed for them to be together too hard and fast. The moment she expressed doubt, he shoved a stone wall between them. Apparently, the knights of Staria did not like to be questioned. It only confirmed she was not the wife for him. Paige would always question.

The rain would not stop her from navigating the forest. Though it wasn't ideal scouting weather, it would hide her tracks. If she could manage to get far enough from the suffocating house, there would be no way Aidan could find her. Any thoughts she had entertained about any other alternative to her situation were just a fantasy. Whether it be in her homeland or in Staria, she belonged in the forest, friend to the trees, sister to the very life and death of the seasons. Even now she felt nature's draw.

Paige pulled the front door open, hoping to slip out of the house undetected. This was the first time since Carrina's arrival that she'd been left unattended in the front room. Gentle drops beat along her shoulder, the sprinkles cool in the evening breeze. Dark magenta light caressed the landscape, giving it an eerie glow.

"I wondered how long it would take you to run," Carrina's voice drifted to her from the side of the house. "I have watched you. I know you have been thinking of leaving us."

Paige stopped, not stepping fully into the rain. Lying, she answered, "You're imagining things. Who said I was running? I just like the rain and wanted fresh air."

"I have watched you. I see what you are thinking," Carrina repeated. She came to Paige's side, staring out over the yard.

"Did the house tell you that?" she mumbled wryly.

"It has been quiet." Then, giving her daughter-by-marriage an accusing look, she added, "I blame you for that. I do not understand why you must resist your fate."

"Of course it is all my fault," Paige muttered, not losing her sarcastic tone. She looked to the heavens, wishing one of the rods of lightning would strike her in the head. From experience, these accusations would last as long as Carrina lacked distraction. "How long until you take to the sea again? I am sure you miss the waves."

"Trying to send me to my death? All in town speak of how you predicted Callum's last moments. Is that what you're doing out here. Watching my death in your visions?"

"Did you say last moments?" A deep sadness stabbed Paige in the chest, causing a sharp pain near her heart. She felt the hints of her dream world falling about her. "Callum died?"

"You saw it in your vision. It happened just as you foretold. The gods swallowed his boat beneath the waves and him with it." Carrina nodded. "It is a very good death for a fisherman. Honorable. Right. His body is where it belongs—in the sea. He would have wanted such an end."

"I don't believe you. There is no way you could know what happened to Callum. You can't go into the village. You don't want to be claimed." Paige wanted the knowing look on Carrina's face to be another one of the woman's wild imaginings.

"With the right disguise I can slip through the streets undetected." Carrina waved her hand in dismissal. "And I do have friends. I was born in Fall-enrock Village."

"I failed," Paige whispered, horrified. "Why didn't he listen to me? I told him to stay out of the water. All he had to do was stay home for one storm."

First, Aidan emotionally abandoned her because she dared to question him, dared to ask for time. Now, her prediction did not help anyone. Maybe the fairies hadn't sent her to the perfect world. Perhaps that was the little creatures' ultimate punishment—to give her hope and take it away.

"You gave him time to arrange what he needed to," Carrina said. "It was a true blessing. He had a chance to make right those things that would have otherwise been undone."

"Blessing?" Paige shook her head in denial, slowly backing away from the woman into the stormy night. The Forestters hadn't wanted to hear about her visions, didn't want her help. The Starians listened, but if they didn't heed her warnings then how was that better? Callum was still dead. She had failed. And with that failure combined with Aidan's distance, she saw all reason for her to be part of this society slipping away.

"Where are you going?" Carrina demanded.

"I need to meditate," Paige lied, smiling in what she hoped was a convincing expression. "Alone."

"Callum had time to say what he needed to," Carrina said, her voice loud so as to be heard in the storm. "His family is grateful. It is a good death."

Paige kept walking, barely noticing the cold rain soaking her clothes.

"You know, the gods did choose you for him. I am surprised you do not see it. The other oracles foresaw it. If he didn't claim someone soon, it was predicted he would have no children. If you walk away from here, everyone will learn of your betrayal and no one in Staria will help you."

"The Caniba..."

"Those beasts?" Carrina laughed. "They would devour you rather than help you. They are not called man-eaters without reason. You would be better off seeking aid from a mammoth wolf."

"I do not need the Starian or the Caniba people." Paige crossed her arms over her chest.

"Come, let us eat," Carrina dismissed the claim. "Your clothes are wet and it is time for the evening meal. You can dishonor the family and run like a coward tomorrow."

Paige frowned and considered her options before marching back to the house in irritation. As she passed the older woman, she mumbled under her breath, "You should know about running, Carrina."

I failed. Callum is dead. I'm a failure.

The thought swirled around her brain in an endless chant.

Failure. Failure. Failure.

Paige had dared to hope that Fallenrock would be different, that here her curse would have meaning. To have that hope taken away with such finality left her all the more bitter and alone. And Aidan's moodiness did little to convince her to stay.

7

"I MUST GO."

Paige looked up in surprise. Aidan stood across the main room, clutching a missive in his hand. He was dressed for riding in a short, plain tunic and breeches. A weapon hung at his waist. His lips pressed together in a long, grim line, a trait that carried itself to his narrowed eyes. She tried to read the emotion in his hard gaze, but only saw anger.

"Where did that come from?" She looked at his hand.

His grip tightened, crumpling the parchment in his fist. "A boy delivered it this morning before you awoke."

"Is it...?" Paige pushed up from where she sat at

the table, abandoning the half-eaten bowl of boiled grains. "War?"

"No." His face gave nothing away.

"Then...?" She took a step toward him, closing the distance.

"It is no concern of yours. I will be gone a day or two." He turned from her, as he had every time she came near him since their fight in the bathing room. "My mother has gone for supplies and will be back later."

A strange sensation prickled the back of Paige's neck but she nodded in understanding. Realizing he didn't see her, she tugged his arm to get his attention. "What is happening?"

Aidan studied her face, his expression searing, as if he might tug her into his arms and kiss her. Her lips tingled expectantly, waiting for more. Instead, he patted her shoulder and stepped around her. "Actually, I may be longer. You should have sufficient supplies until I get back."

With that, he marched from the house. Paige stared for a long moment in confusion. A pat on the shoulder? Like she was some sort of distant acquaintance? And why wouldn't he tell her where he was going? It was clear that wherever he went, it was urgent and important to him.

Paige waited until she heard the sound of horse hooves before rushing to change out of the red and cream gown Carrina stole for her. She slipped into one of the several old tunic shirts and pants she had managed to alter out of Aidan's old trunk. Pulling on a pair of short boots, she armed herself with a knife from the weapons wall.

She didn't bother to stop for food supplies. The forest would supply anything she needed. Outside the weather had cleared, leaving blue, peaceful skies. Jogging through the mushy grass toward the tree line, she headed in the same direction she'd heard Aidan's horse travel. She found the animal's tracks easily in the muddy ground surrounding the forest and took off into a sprint right behind it. The horse would outrun her, but it couldn't hide from her.

As she ran past thick brush and dense trees, leaping over fallen logs and dodging low branches, Paige smiled. The stress of being trapped inside a home began to melt. She hadn't realized how much she missed being encompassed by nature. The thump of her feet hitting the ground mingled with the strange, distant noises of birds and insects. The sounds were a reminder of how much she needed to learn about the creatures of this land.

Paige soared through the air, grabbing a branch to

swing over a particularly rough patch of earth. She skidded to a stop, listening past the beat of her heart for a sign of Aidan's horse. He would have to slow on this treacherous path if he valued the animal's legs. Detecting a distant sound, she turned course, leaving the tracks to cut across the forest.

AIDAN STARED at the small cottage, noting how the once happy home seemed to have become a sad echo of the past. Where once laughter carried on the breeze marked by childish stick fights and Ileen's sweet hold over her brothers, now stood a palpably thick silence.

His horse neighed lightly, drawing his attention to the fact he had been standing for a long time. Forcing his feet to move, he didn't want to face the other side of the cottage door. Until he looked, it wouldn't be real.

The door moved before he reached it and Ileen's face appeared in the small opening. It was real. He saw it in her big brown eyes, glassy and red from tears. Peeter was dead, killed in battle by the Caniba. First he lost his brothers and now his childhood friend. With Paige's declaration of not wanting his children and her doubts as to his worth as a husband, he had never felt so alone. Pain forced its way into every inch of his body, until his muscles ached and his stomach churned. A throbbing settled in his temples, straining the back of his stiff neck. Nothing was as it should be.

The gods curse me. What have I done to deserve such a punishment?

"Dandan," Ileen suddenly wailed, running for him as fast as her small legs would carry her. Automatically, he lifted her up into his arms. A lifetime of training kept him strong and his eyes dry, but inside he wanted to crumple to the ground and scream until his throat was raw.

"Beautiful Leenie," he whispered.

"Papa," she said, that one word revealing her full comprehension of her loss.

"Your father is with the gods. He is a hero who honored you," he murmured. The words only caused the child to gasp shakily before crying once more.

Seeing Shana looking out at him, he walked into the home and quietly shut the door. She reached for her daughter, but Aidan bore the child's weight to the ground since Shana was pregnant. Shana urged Ileen toward the back of the cottage. When they were alone, she said, "They called him to track scouts in the southern marshes."

"Peeter could track a single boar fly in a herd of wild boars." Aidan touched her shoulder lightly and felt her shudder.

"The missive said he found Sorceress Magda's scouts. He and Richard of Daggerpoint were killed taking the Caniba beasts." Shana's lips tightened. He could see the worry and sadness in her face. She cared deeply for her husband.

Aidan knew everything she said and more. His letter from the king would have been more detailed. Even in matters such as these, women were to be protected. Shana didn't need to know Peeter suffered, or that he bled for hours before the gods took him to a warrior's paradise. "His actions will do great things in defeating the Sorceress. Songs will be sung for him. I was told he died well, with great honor."

"I do not need to be told." Her eyes trailed to the back of the cottage, to where her children's low voices could be heard. Her face tightened and her breathing deepened. She rubbed her stomach. "I know their father was honorable. He was a Starian warrior."

"You will have everything you need," he assured her. "Your children will be cared for and your larder full. My mother will help you bring this child when your time comes. I will send her to help you both now and after."

Shana took a step back from him. "Please, do not, Sir Aidan. Not today. Not now." She rubbed her belly protectively. "I know the oracles said you must find a bride, but please, I beg you not today. Not now. I know it is not done in Staria, but my heart is Peeter's. I am still his wife..." She closed her eyes tight and slowly shook her head as if she could erase what was happening.

Aidan frowned, staring at her for a long moment before he finally understood her meaning. "You misunderstand. I only seek to take care of my friend's family. I am not claiming you."

Shana gave a strange laugh of relief, though the sound was filled with a wry grimness and deep sorrow. She surged forth, falling into Aidan's chest as she gripped his tunic. He stiffened at the show of emotion before awkwardly patting her on the shoulder.

"I cannot tell you how you have eased my mind, Aidan." She trembled so hard that the rest of her words were lost.

PAIGE TOOK A DEEP BREATH, then another, unable to calm herself. The run through the forest had been fast and hard, but that wasn't what set her world to spinning. Aidan's horse pawed the ground behind her, but she ignored the creature. He had tied it to a low branch near the forest line.

Staring through the narrow slit in the wall, she saw Aidan's hand stroking the back of a woman as he held her close. The woman laughed, the sound odd and distorted by the way her head presumably pressed into Aidan's chest. Angling her body, Paige tried to get a better view of his face. She knew Aidan was in there, saw his hand.

Who was this woman? Another wife? A lover? A whore? This was why he was in such a rush to leave her?

Paige frowned. It had been days since Aidan found release with her and he was a man of insatiable appetites. Did his abrupt departure mean he was seeking release with this woman? Why else would he hold the woman like that, stroking her back?

Blind jealousy filled Paige and she stumbled back from the narrow window. Her foot bumped into a stick and it landed on the ground with a loud thud. Without thought, she grabbed it and held it tight.

The smooth wood had been carved into the shape of a sword with the end curved to the side.

He claimed her without her permission, brought her to his home, and forced her to tell her vision to a village full of people who would do nothing to stop Callum's death. He made her feel something for him, touched her, kissed her and made her hope. And now, he was here with that woman in his arms.

Paige's heart felt as if it squeezed inside her chest. Hearing a noise behind her, she turned, wielding the stick sword in front of her. Aidan stared at her from the doorway, the woman close to his back.

"Paige?" Aidan began.

Paige growled to stop whatever it was he had to say, but her anger was partially directed at herself for still caring. Even now he took her breath away. Forcing her eyes from him, her gaze traveled down to the very obvious growth at the woman's midsection.

"Paige." This time his tone warned.

She noted the protective way he leaned to the side, hiding the woman behind him. A deep pain radiated in her chest, settling over her heart. Every hope she had allowed herself crumbled around her when she looked at him. Spurred into action, she screamed and swung at the same time. The stick hit him in the side of the leg, catching him by surprise.

Aidan tumbled to the ground. The woman yelped, hopping back on unsteady feet.

"Thirteen children!" Paige yelled, fighting her urge to go to him on the ground, but more so the urge not to hit him again. She saw the passion in the other woman's face, so much emotion and feeling. "I'm agonizing over the fact that your crazy mother insists I'm supposed to give you thirteen children and you're well on your way to a family right here."

Holding his calf, he tried to hobble to his feet. "Paige, halt. Give me the weapon. There is a—"

Paige threw the stick at his head. "You forced me to be your wife. You put me in your home and fill my head with lies about what life is here. Did you think I would not discover what it really is? Did you think me a fool who did not know the ways of men? We have one fight and you run off to—*argh*! And to think I did believe you when you said men here were faithful because the gods demanded it of them. Faithful to yourselves is what you meant. Yourselves and your pricks!"

"Dandan?" A little girl appeared next to the woman and behind her Paige saw several boys. Tears stained the child's cheeks and Paige instantly regretted scaring her.

"Aidan?" the woman asked in shock. "Did she

say she was your wife?"

"Dandan, make her go away!" the little girl demanded loudly.

"No," Paige interrupted, answering the woman. She was unable to look at the girl's watery brown eyes. Paige hadn't meant to terrorize the child. "I am not his wife. I am no one. This has all been a big mistake."

Aidan made it to his feet, but Paige didn't give him a chance to stop her. She ran for the forest, cursing the Faerians, the fairies, the entire land of Staria, Aidan, but most of all cursing herself for daring to believe things could be different here.

Aidan's shouts followed her, but they only made her run faster. Maybe the fairies had successfully punished her after all.

"Paige!" Aidan shouted in an effort to run after his wife. He didn't know what she had heard or thought, but her anger had been clear. His ankle gave out when he tried to sprint and he stumbled.

"Mama!" Ileen shouted. "You are leaking. Dandan, help Mama!"

Chaos erupted, forcing his attention to Shana and her children. The woman grasped her stomach and the ground around her feet was damp.

"Help your mother inside to her bed," Aidan ordered the boys, hobbling toward his horse. "I ride to get help."

As he swung onto the animal's back, he ignored the pain in his leg. The limb wasn't broken and would heal. Aidan urged the beast to hurry, but not in the direction he wanted to go. Hopefully Paige knew the forest as well as she claimed. He tried not to think of the wild beasts that roamed the woods. Mammoth wolves, the monstrous cousins of the smaller prairie wolves, were particularly vicious. Some of the older ones were nearly as tall as a man with the predatory skills to take out a whole group of Starian knights. For the most part, they stayed in the mountain range far to the north, but it wasn't uncommon for them to migrate down when hunting, making their way along the coastline before cutting over to Fallenrock's forestland. Thankfully, he hadn't seen any recent tracks.

Turning his concern to Peeter's wife, he rode to find his mother, knowing she would be outside Martin's house, tormenting the man. After six sons, she would be better equipped to help a woman giving birth than a knight wielding an axe and sword.

HIDING WAS EASIER than she had ever imagined. Aidan didn't even try to come after her. It only proved her point more—he only wanted her when she put up little fight. Apparently, he had a steady woman, and by the looks of her she would soon be back in commission to tend to his needs. She had seen it before—forest liaisons when a man's wife was large with child.

"I just didn't think Aidan was like that," she had whispered to herself more than once. Everything was crumbling, all her hopes for his land. "How could I have been such a fool?"

Evening was darker in the dense part of the forest and she nestled in for the night next to a large tree trunk. The surrounding silence allowed her mind to roam and her thoughts instantly went to Aidan. They started with remembering his face, the tilt of his lips, the open expression he had carried in the bath before they fought. One idea led to another and she found herself moving slowly against the earth. Tree bark scratched at her back, but she pretended it was Aidan's nails raking along her spine. For all his faults and betrayals, the man was an excellent lover.

Then why did he have to pretend there more? He could have just let it be sex. He didn't have to lie. He didn't have to make her feel something for him.

Paige moaned. Aidan had wonderful hands, rough with calluses from years of weapons training. When he touched her, his fingers molding possessively into her flesh, her skin felt as if it were on fire.

Aidan was man enough to stir any woman's desires and the thought caused a wave of rage and passion to consume Paige. She didn't want him claiming another woman or his strong, large body fucking someone else. Who wouldn't want such a perfect warrior in their bed?

She closed her eyes tight, thrusting her hands between her thighs to ease the ache. Even now she could feel the sensation of his cock slipping along her folds, pressing and probing. Losing herself, Paige let go of all control, letting the half-dream, half-fantasy take root, just like when the fairies dosed her with their sexual ambrosia.

"Must have more," she whispered, desperate to have him. "More."

She loved the animalistic sounds he made when he entered her. Paige slipped a finger inside her sex, moving it to mimic Aidan's touch. A blade of grass tickled her shoulder, like his long blond hair did when he thrust above her.

"Aidan," she cried softly, wishing she had the power to make things different between them. Her pussy was wet for him and the bittersweet stroking of her finger didn't replace the feel of solid cock. Her hand brushed along her clit and she met with a gentle release.

Righting her clothes, she turned on her side. The meager pleasure didn't last long as a wave of loneliness washed through her, worse than ever before.

AIDAN WANTED nothing more than to run from the house, from the sound of the newborn baby girl crying. Unfortunately, the midwife threatened to pin him down if he did so much as move. The elderly woman tugged at a bandage, tightly wrapping his leg.

"Do not look so worried, sir," Helen said, coming to the end of her bandage only to grab another one. "I hit my husbands much harder than this and we are still blessed. Today is a day for rejoicing. A girl is born. The prophecy of Shana's children has come true."

Aidan didn't feel like rejoicing, not with Peeter fresh in the ground, not with Paige missing in the forest.

"Peeter should have been here." Carrina appeared in the cottage doorway, carrying a pail of water. "He would have found much pride in the lungs of his new daughter." As she made her way toward the back of the house, past the eyes of the older children, she added, "And the oracle I sent to help you has arrived."

"Oracle?" Aidan's head snapped up and he tried to stand. Helen pushed on his sore leg, making him fall back. Aidan ignored the twinge of pain. "Who? Not...?"

At Carrina's short laugh, he groaned.

"Yea, Sir Aidan, it is I, Oracle Teena." The oracle swept into the room, her long white robes fluttering with her excitable movements. "Oh, look at your poor leg. I suppose I cannot make you perform for me. I will just have to think of another reward for what I've seen."

Out of all the oracles, he could tolerate Teena the least. Aidan glanced at the tattooed bands on his arms—as a guardian of the oracles he couldn't avoid her. Teena's visions were clear, which gave her a kind of queenlike status in the convent she lived in, and the woman used her position to her amusement. The last time he saw her, she made him dance before she would tell him what was in her visions.

"Oh, there now, why don't you smile for me, sir? Or I might not decide to help you." Teena arched a brow. The youthful expression belied her true age. When Aidan managed to pull his tight lips upward into a strained grin, she laughed harder. He wanted to cover her mouth and force her to be quiet. "Oh, very well. I suppose you still blame me for my last prediction. Though I am very pleased you took my words so seriously, methinks you might have gone too far. You only had a few weeks to wait before the breeding ceremony. There was no need to grab the first woman who crossed your path."

"What do you care?" Aidan grumbled. "You said to take a bride quickly or be forever alone. And the old crones agreed with you. I found a bride, I took her. I did what you said. There is no need for me to attend the breeding ceremony to look at bartered brides."

"That is where you are wrong, my dear sir." Teena twirled about the room, pausing to randomly touch this item or that. She hummed to herself, as carefree as a girl child and just as impish. The crying from the backroom lessened, but Teena pretended not to hear the insistent sound. "You will attend the ceremony at Battlewar as you were commanded to do by your king."

"Married men cannot attend," he argued. "I cannot take another wife."

"You question me? Perhaps I will make you dance after all despite your ankle." Teena frowned at him, clearly not liking the fact that he dared to question her.

"And perhaps the next time you are in need of my protection I won't be there." He glared back at her.

Helen gasped, quickly walking from the room as if he had just set it on fire.

Teena watched the elderly woman and chuckled. "I always did love your defiance. I find it quite to my amusement."

"You were saying about Battlewar? How can a married man be a part of the ceremony?"

"Besides the fact the king ordered you to go?"

"Oracle," he warned. "I am very short on patience today."

"Very well." Teena looked at him, but she didn't see him. The dark brown of her eyes began to lighten, slowly turning to a milky white as she peered into his future. Her body shook, her expression fading into a blank mask. Even her voice lost its buoyancy, as she spoke, "Your misfortune is not of my doing, but yours. The gods sent you a bride but you claimed her too eagerly in your haste to get out of the ordained ceremony. You should have taken her with you to Battlewar and set her before the hall so all may hear your claiming. Right now, it is only your word that you staked your claim. The gods demand more from you. They demand that you go to the breeding ceremony and make your intentions known to all. You are a great knight of Staria, a man who is known to honor the gods, and your support of the new brides, even if you do not choose one for yourself, is what the gods wish."

Aidan didn't move, every part of him focused on Teena's words.

"But you ignore the king's order to go the breeding ceremony and you upset the gods by not claiming a bride during the ceremony. Now it is not known if your marriage will be blessed or if you will have children." Teena stopped shivering and her eyes cleared. The haphazard smile returned to her lips. "Why is it so hard for you to believe that the gods reward our men with these women? Do you really think they care how we marry? Your bride's reluctance proves their anger toward you. If I were you, I would send another to find her and bring her to the ceremony where you will reclaim her for all to see. It is your only chance of appeasing the gods, though I do not know if it will be too late for you." Teena began to turn from him only to pause, "And from now on, as a reminder of the gods blessing on the ceremony, all brides must be bound by the hands to signify the binding of the marriage. What is done cannot be undone. It will help these new women understand."

When Aidan didn't readily speak, she arched a brow.

"Rejoice," he mumbled, saying the traditional words, "the oracle has spoken."

"Thank you, Sir Aidan." With that, she turned her attention to the back of the cottage. Walking toward the sound of the crying baby, she began to hum a soft blessing on the home. She did not look at him again.

"MEAT."

Paige blinked, screaming as her foot was jerked and her body pulled from her place on the thick branch. She had been sleeping, dreaming again of Aidan's hands when the rough sound forced her from her bittersweet fantasy.

Her arms flailed as she searched for hold, finally

finding it on a cluster of leaves. She managed to stop her fall temporarily, but another hard jerk forced her to the ground. She yelped upon impact, before knocking her head. Her vision wavered as she fought to stay conscious. A hand caught her jaw, the fingernails biting into her flesh.

An awful smell wafted over her, stinking like the long-rotted flesh of a fallen deer left in the forest by careless hunters. Her vision cleared by small degrees, but she couldn't be sure what she saw was real. Wild, sunken eyes peered into hers from a nest of uncombed hair. The gaze was cold and mocking, yet too intelligent to be a mere creature of the forest. It was a man, but nothing like the men of Staria she had seen. This guy was primitive, unbathed, draped in matted fur pelts.

He began to laugh, showing a mouthful of sharpened, yellowed teeth. "I found meat."

"Caniba," she whispered, the idea hitting her hard. Every nightmarish word Aidan and Carrina told her about their enemy to the south filtered through her mind—*man-eaters, snake people who live in the ground, born of the unholy fornications of people and wolves, the lowest thing a man can become.*

"Meat," the creature-man grunted, the word

drawing Paige's attention to the fact that others moved to join him.

We are far north of the borderlands, Aidan had once told her, *and I promise you I will protect you with my life.*

But Paige had run straight south, traveling for days in the hopes of discovering another of Aidan's lies. She had searched for the Caniba, sought them out. For if Aidan lied about Paige being his only woman, then he had to have lied about the man-beasts.

"Meat," another voice repeated, the sound barely recognizable as a word.

Too late, Paige tried to wriggle free. Her bumped head made it hard to concentrate. Then there was too many of them, hands pressed down upon her, grabbing and clawing, their grips much more painful than the Faerians' had been. She screamed, but the man-beasts only laughed.

They dragged her across the earth before finally heaving her up into a wood and rope cage. They lifted two long sticks off the ground, forcing a strap to tighten and lock her only exit. The cage swung in the air. Paige held on, trying to pull at the wooden bars and twined rope. It was no use. She was trapped.

8

"You should be proud," Sir Edward said, looking up at him from where he knelt on the ground. The words were hardly pleased. "She runs well and covers her tracks."

Aidan shifted on his horse, scanning the trees. "We must find her. We're too close to the borders. I don't like her being so near the Cariba's homeland."

"Gregory's encampment is near, we could stop for supplies and ask if any have seen signs of her." Edward motioned to the east as he strode toward his waiting horse.

"No, she will not go near the camps. She is heading south." Aidan wasn't foolish enough to ignore Oracle Teena's words, but neither could he stand by while he sent Edward after his runaway bride. It was not in his soldier's nature to do nothing. How could the gods expect him to go to Battlewar Castle to await the ceremony? Everything about his beliefs demanded he act, everything in his soul demanded he find his wife.

"Does she not know the dangers?" Edward asked.

"She knows." Aidan refused to say more. How could he admit that Paige didn't listen to him? That she didn't believe him? He absently rubbed his thigh, as if doing so would ease his ankle.

"These tracks are fresher. They head west but it could be a trick." Edward was a fine warrior, one Aidan had fought next to on several occasions. He lacked refinement and had a coarse manner that often bristled the nerves of those around him.

Peeter would have made a better choice to help Aidan in his search, but his friend was gone and Edward was the closest scout available. Despite his rough and rude nature, he was the perfect choice for tracking Paige. Edward would never physically hurt her, he already had a wife and he knew the southern forests and marches along the borderlands. If anyone could navigate into the Caniba territory, it was Edward. And, unfortunately, it seemed that was exactly where Paige headed. "If you are sure she is headed south, we will be better off riding hard for the borders. From there we can sweep back up and try to force her northward."

"I would rather catch her," Aidan whispered so Edward wouldn't hear. "I need her safe."

Edward was right. Paige was good at hiding her tracks, taking to the trees at times, doubling back to throw them off the trail. What she didn't count on was how well Aidan knew the forest. He had tracked his brothers in childhood, endless hours of endless days spent training for their warriors' future. And where his intimate knowledge of the terrain ended, Edward's began.

"It will not be long now," Edward assured him, sighing heavily, as if the chase was barely worth his time. "If she's avoiding the camps, there are only so many directions she can go."

"South," Aidan agreed, falling behind Edward's horse. "As soon as we find her, I'll ride ahead to Battlewar. Tie her up, but only if you have to, just make sure she gets there in time for the ceremony."

"REALLY, I can hunt. I'll bring you food," Paige struggled, desperate to be free of the tight ropes binding her arms to her side. Her legs were tied together, trapping her like a cocooned worm. She almost preferred the sickening swing of her former cage. At least then she had use of her limbs.

Paige's head throbbed, a testament to just how hard she had hit it when the man-beast pulled her from the tree. Heat from a nearby fire inflamed her flesh, not enough to sear, but miserably close. The more she struggled, the tighter the binds became.

Four Caniba men shuffled around the small, makeshift encampment. The firelight cast their ghoulish form with a terrifying light, making them appear bigger and taller. They grunted, their words to each other more animal than man. Bits of flesh clung to their cloaks, the untanned leather the cause of their awful stench. They spoke amongst them-selves, whispering and grunting, only deigning to say to her the occasional, "Meat."

She, apparently, was the meat.

"Please," Paige pleaded, knowing that her words would make little difference. Why had she run so far? She could have been happy in the forest. Safe. She had been so angry, seeing Aidan with that other woman. Now she would do anything to be able to see him again, to talk to him, to hit him with another stick for daring to go to another woman after making her feel something for him. Murmuring to herself, she said, "There is no hope. The fairies have won for this is a cruel and heartless punishment and the Faerians are indeed evil for worshiping such tiny monsters."

She never imagined the little winged creatures would be so cruel as this. Mischievous, yes, even so far as to cause heartache, but to have her end up as the main course in a Caniba feast? Or perhaps this was just fate and the fairies had no idea where they sent her.

Her hands ached and so she did the only thing she could, she began to scream, using all the power in her constricted lungs. The sound caused chaos amongst her captors, but she didn't care. She screamed louder.

AIDAN'S HEART lurched in his chest and he slowed his horse. Reining it to the side, he lifted his hand for Edward to be quiet as he listened. The faint echo of a scream sounded.

"This way," he ordered, spurring his mount past Edward's as he cut west through the forest. From such a distance, he couldn't be sure if the woman was Paige, but his heart beat an erratic rhythm nonetheless. No Starian woman would have come so close to the borders willingly for they knew the dangers and Starian men would have forbidden it. The knights had seen what the Caniba did to their victims and the idea of them doing such to a woman was unspeakable.

The screams became louder, but so did the unmistakable stench of the Caniba. Aidan's stomach curled at the pungent odor wafting downwind. As the tone of the voice became discernible, his heart nearly stopped.

Paige.

By all the swords, accursed woman, why did you run from me?

Forgetting all about the oracle's warning, he drew his sword. His wife needed him to be a warrior. Sweat beaded along his temple as tension filled every muscle. Years of training forced all emotions from his body until his thoughts became a stream of silent orders to his body and all he could do was act.

Dodge tree. Swing blade. Leap onto the good ankle. Save wife.

Before he landed, he had assessed the situation. Paige lay on the ground, squirming. Though they had her bound tight, she screamed at them in rage, thrashing so the Caniba soldier above her couldn't get a good hold. The dirty man held a knife, his crazed eyes torn between finishing what he was about and turning to fight the new intruder. Finally determining Aidan to be the bigger threat, he kicked Paige hard in the gut. Her screaming stopped with an audible cry of pain.

He flicked his sword in one swift motion and turned to challenge the man. There was no need to speak. The Caniba could not be reasoned with for their minds were not like a normal man's. Aidan swung, making contact with one of the soldier's stomachs. Behind him, he heard Edward join the fight, a battle cry on his lips. Metal clanged against metal, echoing over the forest. Determined, Aidan fought his way toward Paige.

PAIGE WATCHED Aidan through tear-filled eyes. Her stomach hurt from where she had been kicked, but the tightly bound cocoon around her body kept her from curling up into a ball. His expression was filled with brutality, his eyes narrowed, his sword moved with swift and deadly force. One of her Caniba captors had fallen to the ground before she could see what was happening.

Relief warred with fear as Aidan descended on the man who'd kicked her. She fought to free her arms but her ties were too tight. Another Starian erupted from the forest behind Aidan, dressed in a hard leather jerkin and dark breeches. Metal diamonds plated the leather, creating a symmetrical pattern over his thick chest.

"You cannot have what is mine," Aidan growled, drawing Paige's attention back to him. A chill raced through her veins at the harsh sound. "You will die for daring to touch her."

The Caniba man circled around Aidan, wielding a chipped knife. There was no fear in the man-beast, no hesitance or prudence. The Caniba warrior thrust his weapon, howling as he charged first. Aidan held himself with confidence, holding firm as he studied his opponent.

The clang of metal hitting metal rang over her. Aidan's friend managed to slit the throat of the man he fought. He strode to where Paige lay on the ground. She expected him to free her, but he merely stood over her to watch Aidan.

She flinched as another loud clash echoed through the forest alcove. A scream of terror built inside her but she swallowed it back. In her struggle to be free, she had inched too close to the fire. The heat from the flames began to burn her flesh and she wiggled away.

The Caniba fighter slashed at Aidan's arm, drawing blood. Crimson wetted his tunic shirt but he didn't stop. Paige looked to the motionless Starian knight standing above her.

"Help him," she pleaded. Two against one would be better odds. Why was the knight just standing there?

The man looked down at her with a snort of disgust. "Keep quiet, woman. You are the cause of this."

She glared at the knight, but he didn't appear to care. Paige's head fell to the ground and she watched, helpless and trapped, as Aidan took another wound to his arm. The Caniba man charged again. She thrashed on the ground, desperate to help Aidan. Her heart leapt in chest as the man swung. Paige couldn't help her scream of concern, "Aidan!"

Deftly, Aidan dodged the blow, surging forward. He knocked the Caniba's knife aside and drove his sword through his enemy's stomach. Next to her, the knight howled victoriously, thrusting his sword into the air. Paige barely heard it as Aidan's eyes found hers. Blood dripped over his hand as he walked toward her.

"Edward, your knife," Aidan said, holding his hand out to the man. The knight at her side gave over the blade from his waist.

"We should ride," Edward said. "There may be others in the forest."

"I have only seen these four," Paige said.

Both men looked at her as if she were an imbecile.

"I suppose there could be more." Paige flexed her hands as Aidan cut her free. She tried to read his expression. He didn't smile at her, but neither was he frowning. Instead, he seemed to look past her, as if he didn't trust himself to address her directly.

Paige rubbed her legs, noting where drops of his blood landed on her breeches. When she tried to stand, she wobbled and almost fell. Aidan's strong hand shot out, steadying her as his fingers curled firmly around her upper arm. Shock waves of heat washed over her at the touch. Her lips parted and she breathed deeply. She tried to speak, but when she looked up into his eyes, he was staring at her. His lips tightened. For a long moment, no one moved.

"I will tend to the horses," Edward said at last, sounding more exasperated than polite.

Paige's heart raced and she realized she held her breath. She forced the air from her lungs, panting as she pried her gaze away from his. A rush of memory came over her, of his hands on her body, his lips kissing her mouth, the way he moved against her. The man was emblazoned on her mind. He had captured her soul and she knew in that moment she would never have run far enough away from him.

"Aidan," she began, licking her lips. "I—"

"Did they injure you?" he asked, inspecting her with his eyes.

Paige shook her head in denial. "No. Nothing I won't recover from."

Edward rudely snorted in the distance and muttered to himself.

Aidan ignored the man. Without further comment, he walked her into a dense, private area of the forest. He favored one leg as he limped, but he didn't let on that he felt any pain. His hand on her arm kept her from dropping to the ground but not from tripping as he led her over fallen branches, slippery leaves and wet grass.

When he finally stopped, his handsome face turned to her. She detected lines of anger marring his tight lips. His eyes narrowed and he looked as if he might speak. His breathing noticeably deepened and she wondered at it.

Paige stiffened. All of a sudden, Aidan leaned

into her. She tried to pull away, unsure if he would strike her. Instead, his lips found hers, hard and passionate. He swallowed her cry of surprise. A thrill coursed through her, seeming to jump off his skin onto hers. Her cry turned into a moan and she grabbed onto his biceps.

His kiss claimed and conquered. He became forceful, clawing at her shirt, jerking it over her head only to toss it aside. Chilly air hit her flesh only to be instantly replaced by his heat. He drew his fingers along her waistband before shoving an insistent hand down the front to cup her sex. Her pants pooled around her ankles. Her pussy was damp, and instantly flooded him with her cream.

Growling, he said, "I burn for you."

Dizzy from the feel of his bold fingers stroking against her, she convulsed against him. Her pussy tightened. Aidan's lips slid down her jaw to devour her neck before moving down her chest. He sucked her nipple, hardening it into a bundle of nerves.

Paige forced all thoughts from her mind. Right now she wanted nothing more than to make love to him in every way imaginable. She rocked her hips against his palm, wanting what she knew he could give her. Massaging her breast, he drew his mouth back up her throat to bite at her earlobe. Small sounds of submission left her throat.

Paige reached for his large arousal, stroking him through his breeches. She unlaced his breeches, pushing them down to expose his cock. Caressing his erection, she kissed his throat before making her way lower. Aidan tossed his shirt aside, finally naked before her. She licked his chest, his nipples, and the indention between his abs.

Sinking to her knees, she kissed the smooth, mushroomed head of his cock. His breath hitched and his hands found hold on her head. She licked him several times, flicking her tongue over his flesh as she sampled his taste. Aidan moaned and his hips jerked ever so lightly. Parting her lips, she kissed the head. His moans turned to pants as she took him deeper with each passing kiss of her lips.

The cold, wet ground cushioned her knees, but she didn't move to stand. His cock was too big to take all the way in her mouth, so she stroked him with her hand, cupping his balls underneath. She sucked him deep only to pull back and do it again.

Aidan jerked. Whatever tension and anger that had taken hold in him soon disappeared under her administering mouth. He rocked in rhythm to her sucking and his fingers tightened.

"My lady, hold. I cannot..." He groaned.

Paige pulled off of his cock at his insistent tug at her head and grinned up at him, licking her lips. Aidan joined her on the ground. He trailed hot kisses down her parted thighs, moving his tongue in small flicks as he neared her clit. His penetrating gaze bore up into hers as he lowered onto her moist slit. She jerked, crying out in pleasure.

He licked her in long strokes as his fingers delved into her wet passage, sliding in the cream that coated his fingers. When she pushed at his shoulder, he only sucked her deeper, thrusting his tongue into the moist cavern of her body. He nibbled and sucked her to the brink of release, only to pull back, denying her.

Aidan crawled over her body, the weight of him pressing her into the ground. She watched him move, mesmerized by the precision of his form. He was a man who knew how to use his body and did so to perfection. Then, suddenly, she saw his cut arm. The wounds no longer bled but crimson trails had dried on his flesh as a testament of his recent injuries.

"Your arm," she said, reaching toward the cuts.

"Is fine," he told her, before she could show too much concern. "But my body is not." He ground his hips into her, as if to prove how badly he ached. His hard cock glided along her slit without penetrating. "Turn around."

She blinked in surprise, unsure she had heard him correctly.

"I want you on your hands and knees," he ordered, the words hoarse. Some of the anger had come back to his gaze and Paige realized too late her mistake in pointing out the wounds. Surely, they only reminded him that she had run away from him, that she had struck him in the leg.

"Aidan, I—"

"Turn around," he insisted, his tone warming.

How could she resist him? Paige turned around, secretly glad to have her back off the colder earth. She looked down to a patch of flattened grass in the shape of her head. Aidan groaned. His cock probed her from behind, pressing along her slit until he found what he was looking for.

Paige thrust her hips back to swallow him inside her. She gasped as he filled her completely. Aidan began to move, thrusting wildly inside her tight pussy, as if he sought to both punish and please her with the force of his claiming. Paige didn't mind. She liked him wild and strong, liked the way he fucked her faster and harder and deeper.

Aidan took her hips, controlling with his hands as

he rode her. Loud grunts of pleasure sounded from him, punctuating each forward thrust. Her own harsh breathing echoed back to her from the ground. She dug her fingers into the earth. Tension built and she stiffened in anticipation, praying he wouldn't stop before she met her release.

Then, finally, she found what she had been looking for. Euphoria erupted inside her sex, spreading throughout her limbs like fire to tinder. Aidan kept riding, forcing her climax to continue. Her pussy clenched him hard. With a resounding yell, he jerked roughly, joining her in their violent release.

Paige's heart beat so hard she feared it might pop out of her chest. Her limbs shook, more so now that Aidan's weight pressed her from behind. When he pulled out and away, she looked over her shoulder to find him limping toward their discarded clothing. She waited for a sign of affection from him, something, a hint of the man he had been with her before. Instead, he began to dress, pulling his tunic over his head.

Paige turned, unable to force her body to move as fast as his. She found her shirt, trembling as she put it on. Aidan tugged on his pants and boots. "Aidan?"

"Get dressed, my lady. Edward will escort you to

Battlewar Castle for the breeding ceremony. I advise you to be careful with him. He is not so gracious as me." With that, he left her to stare after him.

Only fear of Edward finding her naked motivated her to hurry with her clothes. There was nothing to be done about the mud in her hair and on her skin. She tried to brush it off, but it did little good.

After a time she heard footfall on squishy leaves coming in her direction. Edward appeared, a frown etched on his features as he looked her over. "Move it, my lady. I do not send gilded invitations and I am not your mate. Make me come after you again and I will cleave you with my sword and take your head to Battlewar on a pike."

9

"YOU STILL DO NOT UNDERSTAND, do you, my lady?" Edward spat in her direction. Though he called her "my lady" the words held no respect. Not once in their travels had he showed her kindness, often going so far as to tie her up at night so she couldn't run. "Your husband is your master."

"So I should just bow to my husband, without question?" She snorted, purposefully goading his ill humor. Her body was sore, her heart broken and her patience gone. How could Aidan have left her like that? With Edward?

"Yea. When you are chosen at the ceremony by your husband, it is an honor," he paused, looking down at her, "for *you*."

"Good thing Aidan is nothing like you, sir," she

mumbled. "I feel very bad for any woman who you would choose."

"Who said Aidan would choose you at the ceremony? He would be well advised to claim one of the Divinity otherworlders. Their place will have been explained to them. They will know their duty is to submit to their master. They will be good wives."

Paige stopped walking. Aidan would choose another? Didn't he already have another? What of the pregnant woman? Not for the first time since she ran she thought that maybe, just maybe, she had been hasty in her assumptions about the pregnant woman. But that wasn't her whole reason for leaving Aidan. She'd needed to see the Caniba, foolish as that idea was now. She'd needed to know he told the truth and she'd needed time to think about what had happened since being pushed through the fairy ring.

At first, she hadn't thought she would miss her old world. It wasn't like the Forestters were going to mourn her going. But small things began to creep into her mind—the taste of the *gaha* herb in her water, the distinctive smell of the trees that grew near her home, the comfort of the sparse, yet familiar objects that documented her life, being able to visit her parents' gravesites.

"Aidan said that once the claiming was done, it

couldn't be undone," she said, searching Edward's face for a sign he was jesting.

"Normally, yea, but the oracles have proclaimed that, to be official in the eyes of the gods, he must claim you at the breeding ceremony at Battlewar." Edward touched the hilt of his sword and arched a threatening brow. "They gave him the perfect way out and methinks he'll take it."

Paige sighed heavily and began walking again, focusing on hiding her true feelings. Her legs were tired, but she would much rather walk than ride pressed up against the surly knight. On more than one occasion, she had considered hitting him upside the head with a rock. "I cannot believe that all Starian men wish for their women to submit blindly. They cannot all be swine like you."

Edward growled, instantly swinging off his horse. "You will learn respect, woman! Aidan has no reason to choose you, and with his denial you will lose all hope of having status in this world. You'll be poor, at the whim of whoever will take you. But don't look so worried. I will recommend men with a strong hand to silence your tongue. You will learn that your place as a woman is to be subservient—from rubbing your husbands' feet to spreading your legs when any of them demand it, even if they command you to stay on your back all day as they take turns hopping on for a ride. A well-fucked woman is a silent, obedient one."

"You insult Aidan now?" Paige bristled in affront.

"Hardly. No single man, no matter how much of a man he may be, can keep a woman fucked into silence." He looked her over and snorted in disgust.

"I do not need a husband to control my moods, let alone many, Eddie," she protested and taunted at the same time. She knew by the look on his face that he despised the nickname. "And I think that is what bothers you the most. You know my will is stronger than yours. You know that I'm not scared of you."

Edward leaned into her face, his harsh breath hitting her skin and making her sick to her stomach. Paige stumbled back, tripping. She fell to the ground with a hard thud.

"We'll see about that. Mark my warning, my lady. You will be chosen and you will bend to their desires. You won't have a choice. It's either fuck 'em and suck 'em or be cast as a demon spawn incarnate who will be shunned from society, spat on in the streets, locked up and starved like the bottom rung of woman that you are."

"Blazes take you!" she cursed.

"The choice is not yours, lady." Edward spat at

her as he spoke the words. She swiped her cheek in disgust. He chuckled, a dark sound that made her want to knock the teeth from his head. "Resign yourself to spreading your legs."

"Is that a threat?" She didn't like the way Edward was looking at her.

"I have a wife," Edward said, as if that made any sexual threat from him impossible. "But should anything happen to her, you can bet I will not be taking you as my next bride."

Paige felt around on the ground, stopping when her fingers encircled a heavy stone. Gripping it tight, she screamed, surging up from the ground to swing at the unsuspecting man. Her reinforced fist hit his face. Paige jumped back in surprise, not really expecting to make contact with the seasoned warrior. Edward's head snapped back and blood flew in tiny droplets over the side of his horse. Howling in pain, he grabbed his nose as blood began to gush over his lips.

"You cursed whore!" Edward yelled. He grabbed for his sword, partly drawing it as he glared at her. She knew he wanted nothing more than to run her through. To her great surprise, he let the hilt go and the sword slid back into its hold. "The castle is just beyond those trees." He grabbed her arm and threw her toward the horse. "Mount up. I wish to be rid of you."

DAYS BLENDED until Aidan couldn't even count how much time had passed since seeing Paige. All he knew was the ceremony was the following morning and he had prayed to his gods endlessly for a better marriage, a blessed marriage. He had been given the unheard-of option of refusing to take her a second time, but how could he say no? All hope of his future depended on her, of children and of a happy life. The oracles foretold it. His soul wanted it.

Paige was his only chance at happiness in his war-torn life. How could he not claim her again? Even as she dishonored him by leaving him, he wanted her. She could make him go through a thousand levels of Caniba pits and he would still want her, need her, long for her.

Forever. He was bound to her, more surely than a few simple words spoken at a breeding ceremony. When he had been forced to do his duty by Peeter's wife, he had wanted nothing more than to forget duty and honor and run after her. He knew he would find her. Not once had he doubted it. But the idea that he would never see her again caused a fear he had never felt in all his years of battle.

Now Aidan stood alone in the stone worship chamber. Outside wood surrounded the ancient building and inside each sound echoed, amplified so the gods may hear a worshiper in their temple. Columns lined each side, creating an aisle to the front slab table. He had limped the half-day's distance from Battlewar Castle, taking first to the underground passageways then to the dense forest trails, hoping the gods would better hear him in the old place. A horse would have been faster, but he wanted to prove he was humble in his pleading.

Your bride's reluctance proves their anger, Oracle Teena's words filled his head, tormenting him with their certainty.

Aidan forced his feet to move and placed his favorite knife on the slab.

If I were you, I would send another to find her and bring her to the ceremony where you will reclaim her for all to see.

Even now Edward traveled with Lady Paige to Battlewar. He should never have left her alone with the ill-tempered man. But Aidan knew Edward's lack of charms would keep Paige from sweet-talking an escape. For all his roughness, Edward would not physically hurt her.

Aidan frowned, sighing in frustration. He shouldn't have gone to her. He should have slain the Caniba and left without a word like he'd originally planned. But she had looked so scared and he wanted her so much. How could the gods expect him to leave her when she needed him? It was hard enough not demanding to know why she ran, why she struck him.

It is the only chance at appeasing the gods, though I do not know if it will be too late for you.

Why couldn't he have just walked away? Why did he have to risk angering the gods just to kiss her? To touch her? Seeing her tied up like a meal for the Caniba had made him want to hold her, feel her, assure himself that she was unharmed. But he had let it go too far and now he could have possibly cursed himself and his future life.

You upset the gods by not claiming a bride during the ceremony. Now it is not known if your marriage will be blessed or if you will have children.

And so, Aidan bowed his head to his gods, hoping they'd forgive his weak flesh and knowing that he had dishonored himself. Taking the knife, he sliced his inner palm. The pain was superficial compared to the turmoil inside his chest. He then placed his bloodied hand on the slab, letting his blood smear as he began to whisper the ancient plea given to the Starians by their gods when the world was first made.

PAIGE DIDN'T KNOW what was going to happen to her. Edward didn't speak as he rode hard across a prairie beyond the forest toward a city bigger than any she had ever seen. A large wall encircled the giant village and castle. Soldiers walked along the top, guarding those within. Paige didn't know who'd be foolish enough to try to invade such a fortress. Then, remembering the few Cariba she had seen, she shivered. That race seemed crazy enough to try.

A balding knight watched them approach from above the main gate, the only entrance she could see. Only after Edward called up to the man in greeting did he move out of sight. Moments later they were let in. Paige looked up as they passed under, shivering to see the iron-reinforced giant spikes, which made up the bottom of the gate, looming over her head.

Edward led his horse through the narrow streets. Paige searched for Aidan, expecting to see him at every turn. Instead, she found a constant stream of movement as men and women took to the crowded streets. First, there were the peasants' homes, tightly set buildings with no room between houses. She would suffocate in such a place. Remembering Edward's words about her having several husbands to keep her in line, she glanced behind her. Dried blood stained the man's face. Edward growled low in his throat and she quickly looked away.

Paige couldn't help studying her surroundings. There were a couple of barns, many workshops, small breweries and a large marketplace where the commoners sold their wares. Beyond the market, in the center of the city, a second, shorter wall encircled the inner bailey and castle. Contained within were the exercise yard where the knights trained, a small chapel and the stables.

The further they got the more dismal she felt. How could she run and hide in a place filled with so many people? Already she found it hard to breathe. The smells choked her throat and made her lips curl.

Once inside the large castle, Paige began her search for Aidan anew. He was nowhere to be seen, and the more she looked the more her heart ached. Edward had gotten great pleasure in telling her of her duty at the ceremony, of the men who would be there.

Edward grabbed her arm, leading her through a crowded hall. The light came from a large fire box along a far side of the room. Like most things in this place, it was immense and towering. Woven tapestries lined the walls in strips of material, show-casing coats-of-arms and various symbols.

Warriors watched her with interest, gruffly calling greetings to her keeper. Some wore light-weight tunics, others leather jerkins like the guards, others light chainmail and pieces of armor, and still others wore no shirt at all. Muscles bulged, littered with puckered scars and tattooed designs.

Paige tried to maintain a sense of decorum and bravery, but the idea of any of these men claiming her as a wife terrified her—let alone several. As if sensing her fear, Edward told a group of men, "If Aidan does not make claim, she is most willing to be the bride of many. So long as you don't mind sharing, this is the lady for you!"

The words were met with loud cheering. Paige opened her mouth to protest, but Edward jerked her hard and strode with her through the rows of tables, leading her by her arm. Before they made it across the hall, he announced her "availability" several more times, each announcement lewder than the one before it. By the time they left the main hall, she could practically feel the sexual energy in the eyes watching her.

"Aidan," she whispered, willing him to appear.

Edward laughed coldly. "Sir Aidan won't help you. You'll be lucky if he lays claim to you a second time. The man has a chance to be free of you. He saved you from the Caniba and his duty to you is done. Why would he not take it? A soldier like him deserves much more than a whore like you."

"A whore who broke your nose, Eddie," Paige spat. "How about I tell your fellow knights about that? You will not sound so tough having been overcome by a woman."

He growled and his hand tightened. "Come, Lady Paige, let's find you a bath. You will want to be presentable for your new husbands. And if I were you, I'd start praying that they don't tear you apart, because they won't be the gentleman Aidan is. They will fuck you until they have had their fill. Welcome to Battlewar Castle, my lady."

"THE FASTER YOU make them come, the less time you must spend in their presence."

Paige didn't move, didn't let on that she heard the serving woman, Sera. The tight fit of the woman's white corset top squeezed her healthy waist and thrust up two very generous breasts. Long blue skirts billowed around the servant's legs.

After being stripped of her clothing, scrubbed clean by maids with probing hands and not enough sense, scented and dressed, Paige had been indecently questioned by a man named Brock. The man marked her attributes off in his little book like she was an animal to be sold at market. Apparently, if Aidan refused to take her, the others wanted to know why and it was Brock's job to find out. And when she didn't readily answer his questions, he threatened to drag her naked into the hall so the knights could see for themselves that she was "well-formed".

Afterward, she was pushed into a small prison cell with several other women. She had spent the night half awake, trying to drown out their whimpering cries. But how could she blame the other prisoners for their fear? They too were going to be brought out before the Starian men to be claimed. From what she could tell, Edward's assumptions about the other potential brides had been a lie. These women had no idea what they were doing in Battlewar and even less idea of what was going to be expected of them by their new husband or husbands.

Paige was glad that she had at least been afforded a long, shapeless white robe to hide her figure. With luck, these other prisoners would attract the men long before they looked at Paige. It didn't take long for her to realize Aidan was a veritable prince amongst his people. He treated her with respect and honor. She wasn't so sure the others would do the same. Sera's words didn't help to change her mind. Edward had been right when he said she was to be her husband's whore.

"That is all they want—a vessel to find release in," Sera continued, repeating word for word what she had lectured to Paige the night before. The servant eyed the half-dozen girls in the cell as she handed them loaves of bread. "Do not expect tenderness, but if you don't deny them, if you don't resist, you'll be treated fairly enough. And if you give them sons, you'll be greatly rewarded. Life here is not so bad."

It always seemed to come down to children. Paige thought of the men in the hall, her potential "husbands", and shivered. She wrapped her arms around her stomach, trying not to be sick.

"This isn't happening, this isn't happening," a dark-haired prisoner repeated, over and over. "Wake up, Edith, wake up."

"I'm telling you how to best survive this place, please, listen. Spreading your thighs is easy enough a task for a decent life. Don't bring trouble upon yourself. Let them find release. They are not such boars when they get what they want," Sera insisted.

Aidan, don't leave me here. I don't belong here. These women are not like me. They're...

Paige glanced back to the bars, staring past those around her while trying to think of the best word to describe the women. Their mannerisms and speech were so far from her world and what she had seen of the Starian one.

As if to prove Paige's assumptions right, the blonde tried to explain their situation to the crying Edith, "This is another plane of existence you've stepped into. Looking at a foreign dimension is like looking at your world if had it evolved in a different way. To a point there are many similarities. Languages, generally, are relatively similar. Some people will look the same, but not be the same people. Certain events like natural disasters will be shared. Weather is the same and this is still Earth. These people are still human-ish."

MICHELLE M. PILLOW

"You're as crazy as they are," Edith answered, backing away.

While the blonde-haired prisoner tried to soothe Edith's fears, a tall, dark-skinned, black-haired woman gracefully paced in front of the bars as if she might pounce on a second sniveler. Paige turned her eyes back to the bars, absently picking at her wool sleeve. She wondered if the blonde was some sort of fairy. How else was it she knew so much about the other worlds?

The last prisoner, a well-endowed brunette, tried to work a thin metal hair ornament into the prison lock. Suddenly, the woman jerked her hand back and Paige stiffened, hearing the sound of steps coming for them.

"Aidan," she whispered, biting the inside of her lip while she peered to see who came. "Please, Aidan. Come for me."

Paige swore her heart stopped beating when it wasn't him. Why wouldn't he come? Visit her? Talk to her? Let her explain? Let her ask questions? Let her beg him to take her away from this castle.

"Please, Aidan," she whispered, "I don't belong here. Come for me."

A burly man dressed in a hard leather jerkin and dark breeches approached the cells, standing between the bars and the blue-gray stone wall on the other side of the narrow hall. The guard crossed his thick arms, creating a veritable blockade more effective than the iron.

"The flaxen one and the crying one," the man ordered his fellow guards. "They do not carry themselves well. Take them and give them the philter."

Paige sighed in disappointment. The men carted away the two whimpering women, much to the protest of Edith, who pathetically begged, "No, wait! I'll be good. I swear I'll be good. Please, don't hurt me. Please, I'll do anything you want. Do you want me to make you come? I will. I swear I will. I'll do you all!"

"Careful what you wish for," Paige said under her breath, her fingers working even faster to pick imaginary specks from her sleeve.

As soon as the men were gone, the brunette went back to work, her face set as she tried to feel around in the lock with her hairpin.

"You won't be able to open it," Paige said, letting the dejection overtake her. Aidan was not coming. There was no hope. She had been a fool. Staring at the lock picker, she continued, "Even if you did, there would be no escape. You'd have to fight through the warriors' hall, out of the guarded castle gates and run three strikes over open prairie until you reach the forest. Should you survive the wild beasts that live there, you'd soon find yourself prisoner to an even more vicious race of creatures—monsters so fierce and depraved they'll make you beg for death. Trust me, with the war going on in this forsaken place, we're in the better of the two sides."

"Who are you that we should trust what you say?" the brunette asked.

"Name's Paige," Paige answered. These women still had hope. That much was clear. Part of her wanted to dash that hope so she wouldn't have to be alone in her misery.

"Lilith," the blonde interrupted.

"What do they want with us?" The black-haired woman stopped pacing. All eyes turned to her. "Oh, I'm called Jayne."

"They want us to be their whores," Paige answered, bitterness seeping into her hard tone as she remembered Edward's words. "They don't call it that, but that is what they want—a subservient woman to rub their feet and spread her legs. If you don't, they get pissed and the whole lot of them will stare at you like you are the demon spawn incarnate and will blame you for your chosen warrior's bad mood. It's either fuck them and suck them, or you're treated like the bottom rung of Starian society."

"Again, I ask, why should we trust you? We don't know you," the brunette said as she continued to try to pick the lock. "You could be a plant sent here to make us behave, with horror stories of what's beyond the tree line."

"I don't care if you trust me, but I know what I'm talking about. This isn't my first time in a cage." Paige tilted her head back and sighed. At least this cage was big compared to the small wood and rope contraption the Caniba had used to trap her. Closing her eyes, she whispered, "They'll be coming to get us soon."

"What's your name, locksmith?" Jayne asked.

"Karre."

"Well, Karre," Jayne said. "I don't think we have much of a choice. If we all work together, maybe we stand a chance. Now, I don't know how we all got here and at this point I don't think it matters, but I do know I'm not staying to spend the rest of my life as some guy's sex toy."

"I agree." Lilith stood. "We need a plan."

"Fine," Karre grumbled.

Paige opened her eyes and shook her head. "Don't look to me to join your little band. You're only fooling yourselves. I've been to the Hanging Forest. I made it all the way to the Starian borders and I've seen the creatures that wait beyond."

"What about a dimension jump?" Lilith asked. "Does anyone know if this place has inter-dimensional travel technology?"

"A what?" Paige furrowed her brow in confusion. *Inter-dimensional travel technology?*

The women ignored her question.

"Staria? It's too primitive. They don't have the technology here," Karre said. "I got a glimpse of the castle when they brought me to this cell. Through a door I saw servants cart water from a well in buckets and the drive wasn't paved. No artificial lights or motorized vehicles. Though there were several large horses."

"I've never been here," Jayne contributed, "but I'm inclined to agree from what I've observed. These prisons don't use lasers or shocks."

Lasers? Shocks? Artificial lights?

Paige had no idea what these women were talking about.

"Someone's coming." Karre's words kept Paige from asking more. The locksmith pulled her arms out from between the bars. She thrust her lock-picking tool back into her upswept hair.

Paige grimaced to see Edward approaching. He frowned. "Only three new ones?"

"It's all they sent us," the guard answered.

"How's it going, Edward?" Paige queried, keeping her face hard and emotionless. "I see the nose is healing nicely."

"Lady Paige," Edward growled, glaring at her as if he wanted to pull the sword from his waist and run her through.

"Open the door, Eddie," Paige taunted. Maybe if she was disagreeable enough, they'd send her away like the other two. "Let me break it again."

Edward grumbled but didn't answer.

"I thought there were five new." Brock joined his fellow guards. His dress reminded her of Edward, but his personality was less offensive—albeit by a very small degree.

"What's wrong, Brock? Don't I count anymore in your little ledger?" Paige asked.

"You are not new," Brock stated, frowning at her in disapproval. "Your lord is waiting for you and I do hope his punishment is harsh."

Paige's smirk faltered. Aidan waited for her? Mistaking her silence, Brock grinned victoriously. Edward's eyes narrowed and he gave her a smug look, as if to remind her that it wasn't likely Aidan would take her back.

"You already have one of these guys?" Karre whispered, jerking Paige's arm.

"Yes, but..." Paige began.

Karre growled under her breath. "I should have known."

The men left. Accusing eyes turned toward Paige. She shrugged, saying the only thing she could think of. "Ladies, welcome to Battlewar Castle."

"I SAY we make a fight of it," Jayne put forth, twisting her arms in an effort to be free of the ropes around her wrists. She had already put up a good fight as the men came to restrain them in the prison cell. Karre had been no less defiant, though her moves seemed more calculated and her eyes ever watchful. Lilith clearly wasn't the fighter Jayne was, but reminded Paige more of Karre, watchful and waiting.

Paige simply held out her hands and let them bind her. There was nowhere to run and little reason to fight at this juncture. Four women could not overpower the warrior-filled hall Edward had led her through earlier. Besides, the breeding ceremony was starting soon. And as much as Paige wanted to entertain the idea of joining forces with the others and making a run for the forest, something inside her begged her to try to find Aidan. The ceremony was her best bet for talking to him again, to begging him to choose her. Even though she feared he might reject her, a part of her had to believe that he would take care of her as he had often promised.

"Paige already tried fighting and running," Lilith whispered, automatically testing the tight ropes around her wrists. The women made no move to follow the guard out of the prison area. "The way I see it, we don't have any choice but to join forces and pool our knowledge. I think we should gather intelligence. None of us seem to be from this world, so that means they had to get us all here somehow. If we keep our ears open, we'll find out how. There might be a way out of here yet."

Feeling somewhat guilty for her earlier speech of hopelessness and doom, Paige tried to be helpful. Even if she wasn't running, it didn't mean she couldn't help the others. "I've already looked for fairy rings when I was in the forest. I didn't even find evidence of fairies. Though, I'm not surprised. Fairies don't like wars and this place is nothing but one giant battlefield. I think my journey here was a one-way trip."

"Fairy rings?" Karre snorted with soft laughter.

"What?" Paige asked, looking around at the others. "Isn't that how you all got here?"

"No more talking. They're ready for you," the guard announced, motioning his fist forward. "Let's go. March."

Lilith refused to move, no matter how many times the guard demanded it.

"Let me help." Paige tugged on the woman's arm, feeling her shake beneath her hands. Trying to give Lilith the will to take those first steps, she purposefully tried to scare the woman into walking, "Brock's ill-tempered and in the end you'll still be marching out there. Just be glad he's letting you keep the clothes. This is one group you don't want to greet naked."

The other women didn't speak, instead choosing to stay in ominous silence. Paige walked in line out of the prison corridor into the blue-gray passageway. Her heart beat so hard she didn't see her surroundings and barely felt the cold stone on her bare feet.

The sound of the main hall penetrated her thoughts and Paige glanced up to the arched doorway that would take them inside before the eager men. She bit the inside of her lip. How could she let any of these men touch her as Aidan had?

Aidan. Please, choose me again. Don't leave me to many husbands.

Warriors watched the women as they walked in. Paige refused to meet their eyes for fear they might take an interest in her. A slight blush warmed her cheeks and she wondered exactly what kind of rumors Edward had spread about her.

"Come on," the guard muttered when the women didn't move fast enough. His voice did not boom as it had in the prison corridor as he led the brides through a path made between the tables.

Hearing a low growl, Paige glanced quickly to her side. A man reached for her skirt and she quickly sidestepped him. Her actions caused a round of laughter. Realizing averting her eyes wasn't the best plan of action, she glanced over the crowd. She held herself tense and ready to fight off anyone who tried to touch her.

The eagerness in the men's gazes made her uneasy. Those men who had a woman were being pleasured by them in various ways—a stroking hand over their thighs, lips to a neck, a wiggling ass between a man's legs. Tension filled the hall and the talking quieted by small degrees.

"Stand here," Brock ordered, pointing. Paige followed the others to the front of the hall. They stopped before an empty table. It was raised above them on a high platform—a place of honor. Then, yelling, he announced, "Bring in the firsts so they may make their choice."

Noise erupted once more. Paige jolted in surprise at the sudden sound. Then she saw him. Aidan limped in, leading a group of men to the table. She couldn't take her eyes away, willing him to look at her, to smile, to give her a sign that he was going to pick her.

Aidan clenched his fist, looking down over the main hall from the high table. Metal goblets and pitchers of mead and ale spread out before him. Like the rest of the castle, the hall had been designed over centuries of careful planning and fine tuning.

Aidan was one of the six "firsts" given the privilege of first choice. For him, there was no choice. Paige was his. A fact his stiff cock was now very aware of.

Each man wore a different-colored long tunic, reaching to the knees, over tight brown breeches.

Woven belts wound their waists, the end straps hanging along the right thighs. Aidan was glad for the long shirt, as it hid just how painfully he needed his wife.

Seeing Paige, her hands bound like the oracle commanded, he had to force his eyes away and turned to the large fireplace on the other side of the room. It radiated enough heat to warm the hall. The firelight shone through the white of Paige's gown, outlining her slender form in silhouetted detail. His cock stirred, ready to forget everything that had happened if only to plunge into her wet sex once more.

Please, someone claim the shifty brunette so I may take Paige and go, he thought. Because of what he had done, he knew he must wait to choose last. The more he suffered, the better his chances for a happy future were.

Battlewar Castle always made him uneasy. The walls seemed to close in on him and everywhere he went people surrounded him. This time was worse. His fellow countrymen looked at him with a touch of pity and many had already said they supported his decision to not claim the Lady Paige a second time.

A crescendo of laughter and cheering sounded over the hall. The women wore tight corset tops, much lower cut than the women of Fallenrock Village. All of them had husbands who they wiggled enticingly for, some going so far as to sink beneath the tables to give them oral pleasure. Sex was a natural part of life and no one noticed the behavior. What bothered Aidan was the way the unattached men were staring at Paige—as if they could already picture her naked in their beds. He resisted the urge to jump up and challenge them all to a fight to the death.

After seeing some of the more sexual acts happening behind her, he imagined taking her and hauling her away as Ronen had done his new bride, forcibly leading her to his bed where she could service him in any way he chose—taking him into her mouth as she had in the forest, sucking him, pleasing him. And after he came, he would lick her sweet pussy until it was so moist his cock would harden again just for the chance to play inside the tight hold of her cavern.

Lord Ronen and his brother, Sorin of Firewall, had already chosen the first two women, leaving Aidan with Sir Rian, Sir Vidar and Lord Serik. The Divinity otherworlders were to have sent more brides —a lot more—but rumor had it many of the women who'd walked through the inter-dimensional portal had been sent back. It left Paige and a brunette open for claiming.

Aidan looked down the line at the three other men, waiting for one of them to speak. None readily did.

"Oh, all right, I'll start," the brunette said, grinning saucily at the head table. "My name is Karre. I like jewels, riches, power, servants, fine clothes and to be worshiped daily. I also like to get my way. Any takers?"

Sir Rian looked horrified by her announcement and recoiled in his seat. He ran his fingers through his short brown-blond hair before scratching the scar on his cheek.

"Come on, gentlemen, don't be shy." Karre strode before them, carrying her bound arms as if she had been in this position before. "I only bite when I want to."

Sir Vidar cleared his throat and adjusted in his seat. Karre winked at him.

Lord Serik shared a glance with Aidan before shaking his hand. Standing, he said, "I have no wish for a bride. Excuse me."

If Karre was insulted by his sudden departure, she didn't let on. Instead, she started laughing. "Here I am in a room full of warriors and not a one of them is man enough to handle me. I must say this sets a personal record."

"I can handle you." Sir Vidar stood. "Mine."

Karre arched a brow in challenge. "We'll see about that, soldier."

"Rejoice, Sir Vidar has chosen!" the herald announced, trying to hide his laugh.

PAIGE WATCHED Karre follow her new husband from the rowdy hall. She was the only one left. With each second, she waited for Aidan to claim her, to take her out of there. He barely looked at her.

Battlewar was nothing like her home. Everything was too big, too loud and she didn't understand much of what the other brides had to say.

Contact Divinity Headquarters on dimensional plane 269. My employee number is 54367D, Lilith had yelled when her new husband forcibly dragged her from the room. And when Paige mentioned fairy rings, they'd laughed at her. Inter-dimensional travel technology. Lasers. Shocks. Artificial lights.

Paige curled her bare toes against the cool stone floor. She couldn't stay there. She couldn't live anywhere without Aidan. She wanted to go home, to Fallenrock.

Why wouldn't he look at her?

Why wouldn't he claim her?

Paige's lips trembled. She glanced to the side, seeing a pair of narrowed brown eyes on her. The burly knight stared at her chest.

"Mine."

Paige gasped, blinking hard as she looked toward the head table. Aidan stood, limping past the chairs to come around the table. Unsure she had heard him right, she didn't move.

"Rejoice, Sir Aidan has chosen!" the herald said. Audible groans sounded behind her. "Let us drink in celebration. The brides are claimed!"

Cheering erupted and a loud round of toasting commenced, each shout more bawdy and suggestive than the last.

As Aidan came down the platform, she tried to smile. Relief flooded through her. "Aidan," she began, but his look stopped her. A firm line pressed along his lips, casting his features with harsh disapproval. Without a word, he limped out of the hall.

10

PAIGE HURRIED AFTER HIM. Torches along the walls illuminated their path. She ignored the burn of the rope against her skin. The more she moved, the tighter the bindings became. Once they were out of the main hall and away from prying eyes, she hurried through the blue-gray stone passageway, past the wooden doors with thick metal handles spread out on either side. Mazelike tunnels and passages wound around the central hall, each one filled with minimal decorations and landmarks that made them hard to navigate. She had been led through several of them earlier and still didn't know where she was going.

A moan caught her attention and she glanced to the side to where an inlet led to a door. Seeing a knight with his breeches around his ankles, aggressively thrusting between the thighs of the woman he pinned against the wall. Paige stumbled but didn't stop. She quickly averted her eyes, hurrying past. Now that was something she had yet to see in the halls.

For a man who limped, Aidan managed to set a fast pace. She jogged to catch up to him, her bare feet making soft noises on the floor. Paige's bound hands made her movements awkward. "Aidan, wait."

To her surprise, he stopped walking. The noise from the hall had faded, surrounding them in silence.

"You must have something to say to me." Paige studied his back, willing him to turn around. She inched closer, aware of the couple behind her.

"No, I do not, my lady." Aidan tried to walk away. Paige grabbed his arm, lifting her bound wrists to force him to stop. He gave a small hop, changing feet when his weight fell on his sore ankle.

Paige looked down at his foot. "I did not mean to..." She took a deep breath. "Did I do that to you?"

Aidan appeared as if he might not answer. Then he took a deep breath and relaxed. "It was not so bad. It would have healed if I would have kept my weight off it as the midwife suggested."

"I wanted to thank you for coming after me. I should have listened to you when you told me of the

Caniba." Paige heard a loud moan and she glanced back to the inlet where the couple hid.

"You should have," he agreed, drawing her attention back.

Paige's breathing deepened. Aidan's masculine scent drifted over her, as did his warmth. Did he lean closer? Suddenly, her cheeks felt flushed and her heartbeat quickened. Another, lighter moan sounded and she realized it came from her own throat.

"Do you have more than one wife?" Paige asked, thinking of the pregnant woman. "I saw the way you held her, the way you looked at her and the way she looked at you. And the children. Are they...?"

"Shana is without husband," he answered, his voice lowering.

Paige nodded in understanding. A pain took hold in her chest. "She's your mistress."

"She is my friend," he corrected, not denying his connection to Shana.

Friend. Mistress. To Paige there wasn't much difference. Her nose began to burn, but she blinked back her tears. The pain spread, sending a dull ache over her chest and stomach. She wanted him so badly, wanted to touch and hold him, but how did she come to terms with Shana?

Was a little bit of him better than nothing?

Unable to resist, she kissed him, pressing her mouth tightly to his. Maybe she could convince Aidan that she was the only woman for him. She pushed all thoughts of Shana and the children from her mind. If Shana didn't care about the arrangement she had with Aidan, how could Paige feel sorry for the other woman? Paige only felt sorry for herself, for the way her heart broke. Yet, being without Aidan was worse. She had been a fool to think she could leave him.

Instantly, his hands were on her body, gripping the small of her back as he drew her into him. Her tied hands made it impossible to properly touch him back. The light, brushing weight of his cock teased her stomach, easily detectable through the material of her white gown. Her body jolted with desire, warmth and moisture flooding her pussy. Her nipples ached, hardening.

Aidan turned her around so her back was against the wall. She gasped to feel the hard, cold stone. A torch burned over her head, casting his face with a bright orange glow. He tugged at her skirt, insistently urging it up.

"Your ankle," she protested weakly.

"Will be fine," he answered, his words hoarse as he gripped her naked ass. Rocking his hips into her, he let loose a growl. He reached between them, tugging frantically at his laces. "I have more pressing needs, my lady."

It was all the urging Paige needed. She lifted her arms, hooking her bound wrists behind his head. "I didn't think you would choose me again."

"How could I not?"

"Edward said—"

"No, I do not wish to talk of him right now." He sighed heavily before claiming her lips. "All I wish right now is to be in the slick warmth of your body."

Aidan managed to free his heavy arousal. Aggressively he pinned her tighter to the stone wall, angling his cock to strike.

"It would seem the Lady Paige is not so averse to Sir Aidan as we had heard."

Paige stiffened. Her eyes rounding as she turned to look past Aidan's shoulder. He had stopped kissing her, but didn't move. Paige saw the woman from the inlet and her man. The woman stared at them, licking her lips even as she chuckled.

"Aidan." Paige lightly lifted her hands, but kept them around his neck, using his body to shield hers. She urged him to let go of her leg. He did and her gown fell to hide her body.

"You disturb us," Aidan shouted gruffly.

The woman laughed, but the man nodded his head once and grabbed the woman's arm, taking her in the opposite direction.

Paige pushed up on her toes, managing to pull her wrists over his head. Her fingers ached, the numbing pain becoming more prevalent now that the pleasure had been put to a halt. She looked down, flexing her fingers.

"You are bound too tight." He brought her hands to his lips and kissed them gently. "Come with me." Aidan tugged his pants and held them at the waist with one hand and gently pulled her behind him with the other.

Stopping at a door, he knocked, paused, and then walked in when no one answered. Inside, the decorations were sparse, just like Aidan's home. A large bed covered in a big fur pelt caught her attention. Aidan let her go, walking over to a weapons wall to take down a knife. The fire box was barren, leaving the room dark but for a stream of light coming from a narrow slit in the wall. After the bright passageway, she had to blink several times.

"There are animals like that here?" She gestured to the pelt.

Aidan glanced over, nodding. "The mammoth

wolf. They come down from the mountains." He sawed the knife against her wrists, deftly freeing her.

She sighed, flexing her fingers to draw the blood back into them. Going to the pelt, she touched the fur. "Do you hunt them?"

"Yea."

"Will you take me to see them sometime?"

"Perhaps." The sound of Aidan sitting on a cushioned seat caused her to turn. The laces at his waist were still unfastened from their time in the hall. He tugged on his boots, tossing them aside. Her eyes strayed to the bulging cock still hard and ready.

"I'm sorry I ran. I'm sorry I hit you." She took a step closer, lowering her jaw as she studied him.

"You said that already."

"No, I said I wanted to thank you for coming after me and I should have listened to you when you told me of the Caniba." Paige gave him a small smile.

He dropped the second boot and leaned back. His arms rested at his sides. "Why did you run?"

"How could I not?" It wasn't an answer but she didn't know what else to say. I'm sorry? You should be sorry? I saw you with her and I couldn't think beyond it? After days spent worrying that he may not want her again, she was in no mood to have her heart broken by discussing it in detail. "May we speak of it later?"

"If you wish."

Paige bit her lip as she went to him. "Where were we before we were interrupted?"

Aidan lifted his hand, lightly tracing over her red-tinted wrist where the rope had rubbed into her flesh. "Take off your gown."

Paige lifted the simple garment over her head and dropped it aside. She stood naked before him as his narrowed eyes slid over her body. A slow smile curled his lips and Aidan reached for his tunic shirt, pulling it off and tossing it aside so his chest was also bared.

She shivered, kneeling before him. He watched her with narrowed eyes. Inching forward between his thighs, she let her fingers skate up the muscles of his legs toward the thick arousal straining against his breeches. Paige licked her lips, slowly drawing her tongue to wet the flesh. His gaze roamed to her breasts and soon his hands followed, cupping them, teasing the nipples. She closed her eyes and sighed, as she leaned into him.

The laces were still undone and it didn't take much to pull his pants from his hips. He lifted off the seat, letting her undress him as she slid the warm material down his legs and off his feet. When she had him naked, she kissed his knee, leisurely moving to his hip, pausing to bite at his side. Aidan moaned, stiffening slightly.

Paige moved her mouth to take his cock between her lips. She kissed the tip before tracing her tongue along the ridge. Slowly rolling her mouth forward, she sucked gently. Aidan brushed his fingertips along the back of her ear as he lifted his hips to thrust deeper into her mouth.

With a deep groan, Aidan hooked her beneath her arms and lifted her up onto his lap. His chest rubbed along her nipples. His strong hands moved over her back, protective yet masterful. The blond length of his hair tickled her shoulders.

He explored her ass as she ground against him. The words strained, he said, "Take me inside you."

Paige lifted over him only to plunge down, impaling her body on his cock. She inhaled sharply, letting his hands guide her as he lifted her up and down, up and down, in an endless progression of perfect movement. Her legs hit the arms of the chair, keeping her body from taking him as deeply as she wanted to, but the friction felt too good to stop and reposition.

She let her head fall back on her shoulders as

Aidan drew her breasts to his mouth. He sucked a nipple between his lips, moaning into her. The tension built, causing her to increase her pace. He grabbed her ass, rolling her forward on each down thrust. His lips slid from her breast and he groaned heavily so that the noise echoed all around her.

Suddenly, he pushed up from the chair, taking her with him. Paige wrapped her legs around his waist to keep from falling as he carried her toward the bed. Almost roughly, he dropped her on her back. Her legs hung over the side, still hooked to his waist. Aidan came over her, eagerly searching to reenter her slick passage. His hands pressed along her sides. Bracing his feet on the floor, he took her hard, rocking forward into her ready body.

Paige kept her legs around him, spurring him on. The tight muscles of her pussy clenched him, holding him deep. He withdrew to the opening of her sex, only to thrust once more. She tightened her legs, keeping him deep. Aidan began to stroke her core in shallow thrusts. She jerked in pleasure, clawing at his arms to urge him on.

Soft fur cushioned her back as his heavy weight held her down. Aidan caught her nipple between his teeth, biting lightly before letting go. Then, reaching between them, he massaged her clit in tiny circles.

"Ah, please," Paige begged, needing the wonderful torment to end. She became trapped in a mindless web of ecstasy and thought her mind might explode with the intensity of it. Then, finally, she met with blessed release. Tremors raked across her entire frame, until her hand weakly dropped down his arms, barely able to keep a hold of him. Inside, it felt as if her bones melted.

Aidan's climax soon followed and he shuddered above her. With a light moan, he dropped down on his elbows, pressing his forehead to hers. For a long moment, they didn't move, only shared in harsh breaths. He moaned lightly, rubbing his lips to hers in a gentle kiss before pushing off her.

Aidan crawled onto the bed, lying naked on top of the fur coverlet. He wound his hands behind his head, closing his eyes. Paige joined him, stretching out next to him. He sighed heavily, saying, "This is not your world. No matter how much I want it to be, it is not."

Paige thought of Battlewar—overcrowded, overbearing and filled with strange unpleasant smells. "No, this place is not."

When he looked at her, a deep sadness filled his eyes. He turned on his side and caressed her face. "What if I told you there was a way for you to go home to your world? To rejoin the Forestter people?"

"You know of a fairy ring? I found none in the forest."

"I know of an inter-dimensional portal, a strange machine that will somehow take you home to your plane. All you have to do is walk through it." Aidan glanced away from her and back again. "It is beneath the old dungeons of this very castle. I can take you to it. I will contact the Divinity otherworlders and ask them for the directions to your home world. We can remain here until they find which plane is yours. If that is what you wish."

Paige sat up on the bed, curling her arms around her knees. Her fingers worked against her flesh as she hugged herself tightly to keep from shaking. "You want me to leave? You claimed me so you could send me home?"

"No. I will admit, sending you home was never my intent. I truly believe the gods sent you to me, to be mine. I would hold on to you forever if you agreed to stay as my wife. But I have come to realize that I cannot force you." He ran his hand up her back, following her spine. "You chose an unknown life in the forest over being my wife and faced nearly being devoured by the Caniba beasts. If you are truly so unhappy, I cannot make you stay with me."

"Those other women in the cell talked about an inter-dimensional portal, but I didn't understand most of what they said. They acted as though they stepped through fairy rings all the time."

"It is how they came to be here. The people who sent them call themselves Divinity Corporation. They made their own fairy ring to travel through. They do not wait for fairies to bring them to the right world. They travel like we would jump across the room, leaping from one world to another with ease."

"Why?" Paige frowned, unable to think of any practical reason to hop through worlds like that. "Did they lose someone through a real fairy ring? Do they need hunting land?"

"I believe they are traders. They wish to give us women in exchange for water." Aidan furrowed his brow in thought.

"Then, they have no water on their land." Paige nodded. That would make sense. "They try to save their people."

"Methinks their missions are not so noble. They only wanted samples of the blue mineral water, not drinking water, and not enough to save a whole world of people." He drew his fingers along her back, as if writing on her like she was a piece of parchment and his finger the pen. "Their logic is flawed, their reasoning faulted. You saw the women they brought to us. Two had to be given a philter to knock them unconscious before being sent back to Divinity."

"I saw them." Paige thought of her night in the prison cell, trapped with the terrified women.

"It is as I've told my countrymen from the first. Brides cannot be brought to this land by force just because we want them. They must be blessed and sent by the gods in reward for a man doing his duty."

"Those two cried all through the night and one even started yelling." She rubbed her ear, remembering the high-pitched, incessant screams. "I'm inclined to agree with you. Brides should not be forced."

"I understand what you are saying." Aidan's hand stopped and he withdrew it. "I will make arrangements to send you home."

"It might be best if I did," Paige answered, unsure how she managed to get the words past her lips. Part of her wanted to run, part of her wanted to stay. Here was her chance to go home, but she found she wasn't ready. But how could she stay knowing what she did about Aidan and Shana? Just thinking the woman's name brought back that expression on her face—the agony, desperation, love, so much raw emotion as she clung to Aidan. When he didn't say anything, she added weakly, "I do miss a few things."

Aidan merely nodded, not speaking. When she looked into his eyes she couldn't think of what those things might be.

"I miss the tastes and smells. I miss listening to festival music from the trees." Small things, all things that she could live without.

He looked down at his hand, studying the edge of his fingernails. "Is there a man waiting for you? You never said."

Paige gave a cheerless chuckle, shaking her head in denial as she thought of how she scared off any suitors merely by being alive. "No. There is no one."

"Then you won't consider staying, of seeing if you enjoy being my wife? I promise to honor you. I will take care of—"

"Aidan, it's not that. I know you're honorable by all the standards set by your people, but I cannot share you with your friend. I saw the way she looked at you, the way they all looked at you."

"All?"

"The children. A father should be with his children."

Aidan began to chuckle. At first it was small, but

it quickly grew into a hearty laugh. "You think you have to share me with Shana?"

Paige studied him. "Shana isn't your lover, is she?"

"Lover? No." Aidan sobered some, his smile dropping. "She is the wife of a friend who died following Caniba scouts. It is my duty to help her and Peeter's children."

"That was the reason why she looked at you like that, with so much emotion. She lost her husband. I thought..." Paige closed her eyes. "I thought that emotion was for you."

"And that is why you ran." It was more of a statement than a question.

"Yes. I saw you with her and—"

"You struck me." Aidan lifted his ankle, showing her a fading bruise.

Paige leaned forward, crawling so she could lightly kiss his leg where she had hit him. Then, lying on her stomach, she skated her fingertips along his shin. "I don't want to stay here."

"I understand. Tomorrow I will send word to Divinity."

Paige dropped her hand and glanced over her shoulder. "I mean, I don't want to stay at Battlewar. The village is too big. I find it oppressive."

"Where do you wish to go?" He sat up on the bed, touching the back of her thigh.

"Back to Fallenrock." She concentrated on drawing random patterns on his calf, careful not to touch the bruise.

"You wish to stay as my wife?" His hand moved higher.

"I wish to stay," Paige said carefully, "and see what happens between us. Why must we rush into marriage?"

"You wish for two fortnights filled with intention courting?" Aidan massaged her ass, deeply rubbing the muscles.

Paige closed her eyes, enjoying the intimate attention. "You remember?"

"I remember everything you say," Aidan said. "Your people have two fortnights filled with intention courting and then exchange blood to seal a union. We have satisfied my people's rituals. If I must satisfy yours to prove to you that I am your fate, then so be it. I will gladly face the challenge."

Paige licked her lips, smiling. It touched her that he would honor her traditions.

"My first intention is to kiss you here." He leaned over, pressing his lips to the back of her thighs. His fingers continued to massage. "And here."

Paige jerked when his lips brushed lightly over her ass cheek. "That is not how intention courting is done." She turned to look at his face. "You have to state your intentions."

"I am." He grinned. "I intend to kiss you here." He kissed her hip. "And I intend to kiss you here."

"Those were not the intentions I speak of. You have to come to my doorstep every day with a gift. Normally, you would speak to my parents first, but since they have passed and I have no guardian..."

"Then I can kiss you here?" Aidan nipped at her ass cheek.

"You are not allowed to kiss me at all."

At that, he frowned and sat up. "You jest."

"No." She shook her head. "It's a time when you state your intentions."

"But, we can still...?" Aidan lifted a brow meaningfully and glanced at her hips. "Yea?"

"No." Paige couldn't help laughing at his look. As much as she wanted to lean over and kiss him, she knew that she needed him to face this challenge to prove he really did want her for more than easy sex. She pushed up on the bed.

"But, I will not use my lips," he swore. Covering his mouth, he said from beneath his fingers. "No kissing."

"Come, Aidan, take me back to Fallenrock." She reached for her white bridal gown and slipped it over her head.

He grumbled, pushing up from the bed. "Fine, but only because we can do nothing else."

11

"I WILL TELL everyone what you are doing," Carrina said, pointing a bony finger at Paige. By the look on her face, one would think Paige was a traitor to Staria. "How do you expect to have thirteen children if you do not let your husband touch you? There is something very wrong with you. Very wrong."

"Blessed morning, Carrina." Paige yawned in greeting, stretching her arms over her head as she walked past Aidan's mother. The warm glow of morning sunlight called to her and she headed outside. Well, if she was perfectly honest, the warm glow of Aidan's naked chest as he did his morn exercises called to her more.

"Very wrong!" Carrina yelled after her. No matter how many times they explained their arrangement to the woman, Aidan and Paige could not convince her there was nothing wrong in their marriage.

"All right," Paige said absently over her shoulder, not really paying attention. She wore a new gown, made for her by a seamstress from the village. The cream-colored linen underdress with a brown and tan striped corset bodice was her favorite.

The first fortnight of intention courting had been rough. They rode on separate horses from Battlewar Castle to Aidan's home. With the aftermath of their coupling so fresh in their minds, they were able to resist that first night. The next couple of days were harder. Aidan's hot gaze made her almost give in, but he respected her and kept his distance. The days after that, he started gravitating closer to her, sometimes to the point she could feel the heat of his body looming close.

It was pure torture.

The second fortnight began with Paige biting her lips to keep from crying out as she pleasured herself in her lonely bed. Her fingers felt good, but they weren't Aidan. She missed his touch.

Yet, for all its torment, not touching had its advantages and she began to see the logic of her Forestter ancestors. Staying apart forced them to find other ways of spending their time together. They could speak without falling into passionate kisses. Aidan told her of his brothers, of Peeter, of the pranks they pulled on each other while waiting for battle. He brought her gifts—mostly throwing knives and daggers. Though, he did bring her a bow and quiver of arrows. Paige still got giddy thinking about the fine quality of the weapon, even if he never gave her a straight answer about taking her to hunt one of the mammoth wolves.

"I believe your mother plans on feeding us her special food again. She has that look on her face," Paige said, coming around the side of the house. "How anyone can be in the mood to do anything after eating such a horrible concoction is beyond me. It is about as tantalizing as talking about bearing thirteen children. Do you know she told me the other day that she thought nineteen would be better?"

"She only says such things to get a rise out of you," Aidan dismissed. He swung his sword before him several times, thrusting and twisting as he took on an imaginary opponent. He began moving with more vigor than usual, his face tight. "I will speak to her and tell her you do not wish for children."

"Who said I do not want children?" Paige frowned.

"You did. Often. I told you I listen to what you have to say."

He was right, he did listen, but clearly he had misheard. "I said I did not wish for thirteen children. Why must it be none or many? In my world two is considered acceptable, four many. Thirteen is unheard of."

Aidan stopped, lowering his sword while he studied her. Sweat glistened on his neck and chest, gluing strands of his hair to his back and shoulders. He breathed deeply from his exertions. "Four?"

Paige laughed at his hopeful look. "We'll see."

"So, does this mean you are agreeing to stay here as my wife?" He dropped his sword on the ground, striding toward her. Lifting his hand, he made a move to caress her cheek, but stopped midair. Paige turned her cheek into his palm, but he drew it aside. "We still have one more day."

"Are you sure your count is not off?"

"It is your custom, not mine," he said.

"I say we are properly courted." She tried to lean into his hand again, but again he pulled it away.

"It is my custom to prove to the gods I am worthy." He dropped his hand and stepped back. His eyes held liquid promise as he licked his lips. She shivered, the rush of denial overwhelming her senses.

"I will not fail so close to my goal. no matter how hard it is to not touch you."

Paige lifted her hand, letting it hover close to his face. She felt his breath on her palm. Heat radiated from his chest. "I do not think I can wait."

Aidan glanced around. "Come with me." He led her toward the stables, going behind the building. A dense overhang of trees brushed up against the back of the building, creating a private alcove. Aidan kicked off his boots and turned to her, keeping distance between them. He tugged at his waistband, unfastening the laces. "Disrobe."

Paige glanced behind her.

"Take off your gown. Let me see you," he insisted.

Paige slowly tugged at her laces, wondering what he had in mind. She smiled, thinking he meant to claim her here and now. The thought made her fingers quicken their task as she jerked the corset over her head. The linen underdress soon followed. Warm air tickled her naked flesh, arousing her already taut nerves. Her nipples hardened, puckering into needy buds. She tossed the gown over a tree limb before facing him.

When she tried to go to him, he held up his hand to stop her progress. Aidan stood naked before her, his gorgeous, flushed body tight with muscles. Spots of light shone on him through the trees. His cock lifted, full and thick from the long, seemingly endless days of denial. He ran his hand down the center of his chest. His eyes focused on her breasts.

"Touch them," he said, the words low. "Let me watch."

Paige, understanding his meaning, reached for her chest. She rubbed her breasts in slow, pleasurable movements. Her breathing deepened as arousal focused where she touched. Aidan's hot gaze and panting mouth captured her eyes. He touched his own nipples, mimicking her movements.

Paige pinched her nipples and gave a low moan. Aidan's hand instantly went to his arousal to fist the length of his cock. She watched him stroke it, never having seen anything quite so erotic or arousing in her life. Her hand seemed to have a mind of its own as her fingers glided down to her sex. She parted the folds, jolting visibly as she brushed her clit. Gasping, she did it again.

"Aidan, please," she begged mindlessly. "Let me touch you."

"Touch yourself for me," he commanded hoarsely. "Let me watch you come."

Paige stared at his cock, licking her lips. She

continued to finger her clit and fondle her breasts. Her head became light with desire and she wobbled on her legs. "Please, Aidan, I need you inside me. I need it. I cannot take any more torture."

He looked like he wanted to give in, but instead said, "We cannot. We have one more day."

"It's been so long," she cried. Rocking her hips against her hand, she massaged her clit. "At least give me your hand. Let me ride your fingers. Or your mouth. I want to ride your tongue. Oh please, kiss me, suck on my pussy."

"Get on the ground," he panted, pumping his fist hard and fast.

"Oh yes!" She licked her lips, getting on her knees. "I'll go first. I'll suck your cock." Paige opened her mouth, ready to taste him.

"You know how to tempt a man, my lady," Aidan growled. He took a step for her.

"Yes, come here. Give it to me. Give me your cock."

"Lie on your back," he said in a rush, each word more frantic than the last. "Spread your legs so I can see your fingers going inside you. Let me see what I have suffered for."

Paige groaned, realizing he didn't mean to touch her. However, she obeyed and got on her back, opening her legs wide as she slipped her finger into her wet, aching pussy. Suddenly, her body could take no more and she came. Her muscles seized with pleasure and she could barely move as she let the pleasure rack through her.

Aidan stood over her, pumping his cock. "Oh yea, so beautiful, so wet. I want to fuck you so badly. I want to taste your cream. Let me see you taste it."

Paige brought her fingers to her lips and tasted herself. Aidan jerked, spilling his seed on the ground between her thighs. He sunk weakly to his knees.

Paige turned her knees inward, staying on her back as her heart began to slow. Aidan drew his hand along her calf, keeping it from touching as he pretended to caress it. She rolled her head back on her shoulders, looking up at her dress hanging on the limb. The breeze pushed it gently over her head only to let it drop back on the branch. "I'm not sure if I feel better or worse."

"Perhaps I should go hunting today," Aidan said, eyeing her naked form. "Alone."

"Perhaps you should," she agreed, sure she'd not stop herself from attacking him should he try to initiate another no-touch sexual encounter. Standing, she tugged her gown off the tree and began shaking out the long folds so she could redress. Absently, she considered her day and said, "And perhaps I will try to get Carrina to visit Martin. I might drag her in front of him so he can finally claim her."

"She does not wish to be claimed," Aidan said, a little defensively. He tugged on his pants.

Ah, men and their mothers, Paige thought wryly. "Since when has that fact stopped a Starian man?"

Aidan frowned and Paige instantly wished she could take the words back. She didn't mean them as harshly as they sounded. "It is not the same thing."

Paige pulled the gown over her head to keep him from reading her doubtful thoughts. She had plenty of room to make argument, but refrained. "Perhaps she wants to be caught."

"Do you wish to be caught?" He arched a brow.

Glad to see his playful mood, she said, "It depends on what you bring me tomorrow, mighty hunter. Ask me again then."

"So you are the new oracle." Oracle Teena's dark brown eyes focused on Paige, sweeping up and down. Aidan had told her stories of the woman. At the time she thought he exaggerated about the woman's sanctimonious attitude. "We are quite insulted that you have not been to the temple to visit."

"I was not aware I needed to go to a temple." Paige crossed her arms over her chest. The woman had been waiting inside with Carrina when she came back from her semi-tryst with Aidan. Outside, she heard the sound of his horse riding away. He already left to hunt.

"A new oracle comes to join us and you do not think it warrants a visit?" Teena clicked her teeth. She walked around the room, holding her arms away from her body so her long white robes fluttered behind her.

"I did not come to join you. I was sent here by mad fairies." Paige turned her full attention to Carrina. "You arranged this meeting, didn't you?"

"Methought you could use Oracle Teena's help," Carrina said. "If you will not be a wife, you can be an oracle."

Paige gasped at the bold words in front of a stranger. "Who says I'm a wife? How many times do I have to explain it to you?"

"So you prefer to be a camp follower?" Oracle Teena asked, smiling mischievously. "I am afraid the oracle council will not allow that. You have been claimed and by a guardian. There are worse husbands to have."

"You should listen to her," Carrina said. "Her visions are some of the clearest."

"It is my pleasure to help." Teena preened at the compliment. "But, it is true. I predicted your coming for Sir Aidan. The fact that you have problems in your marriage is no fault of mine. He was instructed to go to the breeding ceremony but he claimed you too soon. I had a feeling he would."

"Sure you did," Paige drawled. She really wanted to grab a chair and throw it at Aidan's mother. With a deep breath, she refrained.

"I know what you're doing. Of your custom." Teena gave a small, condescending laugh. Looking at Carrina, she said, "Could you leave us, lady? Perhaps you should take to the forest. Methinks Martin comes looking for you."

"Thank you, Oracle Teena," Carrina said, interest lighting on her face as she ran outside.

"He's not," Teena said when they were alone, "but Carrina enjoys the game."

"What do you want with me?" Paige asked, not liking the condescending way the woman presumed to know her and her life.

"Me?" Teena waved her hand in dismissal. "Nothing."

"Well then, it was a pleasure to meet you. Safe journey home." Paige made a move to leave.

"Wait." Teena frowned, her tone becoming dark and irritated. "I can see you are one to talk of points."

"I do not even know what that means."

"Let me be direct. We want to know what your gifts are." Teena crossed her arms, losing the graceful fluttering she'd shown before. "How did you know of Callum's death on the sea? No one else saw it."

Paige took in the woman's expression. "You want to know if I'm better than you."

Teena's face reddened. "This is about Staria, not me."

"Sure, it is." Paige shook her head. "I see it all over your face. Let me guess. You are the type who is used to people acting like Carrina, never questioning you. But, me, I do not know you. I am not scared of you or your predictions. It's easy to say you saw me coming and you knew this would happen, but if you really want to impress me, tell me something that is not old news."

"Very well." Teena closed her eyes briefly. When she opened them the brown had faded to milky white.

Paige took a step back in surprise. "What are you doing?"

Teena's expression faded and her body shook. Blankly, she droned, "You should not be angry at me for your mistakes."

"My mistakes?" Paige demanded. "What gives you the right to—?"

"Aidan has proved his worth to the gods, but you have not. This marriage is blessed, but the gods may have more trials for you."

Paige arched a brow. Teena stopped shaking and her eyes cleared.

"That's it?" Paige asked, snorting with laughter. "What in the green of the forest am I doing listening to this? That's the best you have? A vague premonition that the future might hold trouble for Aidan and me? You could say that about anyone. You call that impressive?"

Teena's forehead wrinkled in anger. "Well, I-I-I—"

"Let me help." Paige let go of all control, allowing the rush of feelings and images into her soul. She let the wind carry her through the forest, past trees with broad leaves and fat trunks, by red-tinted shrubs, over trickling brooks lined with rocks and the acorn-littered ground. Then, like a burst of sunlight, she felt warmth overtake her entire body. She saw Aidan looking at her, reaching for her, smiling at her as if the expression was permanently etched on his features. But it wasn't his face. It was the face of an old man who had his eyes and his smile. Gray had overtaken his blond hair, now shortly cropped, and wrinkles carved his face.

"You have always had my heart, my lady," Aidan whispered, his voice raspier than she knew it to be. The breeze swept her mind around him until he overwhelmed her senses and in that moment she knew that all would be well. Paige breathed heavily as she was jerked from the moment. Never had a vision been so vivid and real.

"What?" Teena demanded. "What did you see?"

"The gods may have trials for us," Paige answered, grinning, "but we are definitely blessed."

"That is what I said!" Teena protested. Paige took her by the elbow and escorted her toward the door. "But you did not say anything that I did not see—"

"Good journey, Oracle Teena," Paige replied. "I'm sure I will see you again."

"But, your gifts? You have not told me of your—"

Paige shut the door, cutting off the oracle's words. She didn't know about the Starian gods' blessing or her family curse. She didn't know if Teena spoke the truth or was completely mad. All she knew is that she had seen into the future and it was more than she could have ever hoped for.

Sweet feelings of hope and excitement flowed through her. She looked around the home with new eyes, feeling as if she had finally found the place where she truly belonged.

12

PAIGE NERVOUSLY FINGERED the blade of the knife she had taken down from the weapons wall in her bedchambers. The double-edged dagger had finely carved scrolls down the center ridge of the blade, which led to a pointed tip. A silver pommel carried the same fine carving and black leather strips wound around the hilt.

All day, nervous excitement coursed through her veins and time seemed to go so slowly she thought she'd go mad from having to wait. She had even gone so far as to help Carrina clean the long line of rooms along the hall. They were the old bedchambers of Aidan's brothers and covered with a fine layer of dust.

Not even Carrina's sour looks and disappointed

grimaces could mar Paige's happiness. She had seen her future and it looked wonderful. Even old, with wrinkled skin and grayed hair, Aidan made her heartbeat quicken. And his words. Oh, those wonderful words.

You have always had my heart, my lady.

She wanted to jump up and down every time they echoed through her mind. He'd never said anything like that to her before. But then, why would he?

You have always had my heart, my lady.

Paige winced, accidently cutting her fingertip on the sharp blade. Sucking on her hurt finger, she walked from the room.

"Paige?"

Her heartbeat sped to hear Aidan's voice. She hurried down the hall toward him. The soft glow of orange light from the fire box illuminated his face as moonlight silhouetted him from the opened front door.

"A new gown?" He motioned at her green dress. The bodice was a darker shade than the under tunic.

"It came today from the village," she answered.

"Hm." He nodded in approval.

"How was hunting? Did you bring me something?" She pressed the pommel of the knife into her palm, rubbing it in small circles as she was careful not to cut herself again.

"I did, but I do not think you want to see it, at least not in that gown." When he came closer, she saw his hair had been washed and slicked back from his head. Seeing her attention, he ran his hand over his hair, explaining, "I stopped at the creek."

"Your mother asked Oracle Teena to stop by," Paige said, trying to lead the conversation toward her vision. She looked at his face, trying to contain the eager hope she felt at remembering her vision.

You have always had my heart, my lady.

"I must apologize for that, my lady. Oracle Teena is, ah..."

"Exactly as you described her," Paige said. Aidan didn't reach to touch her. Paige couldn't take it. She dropped the knife and surged forward, throwing her arms around his neck.

Aidan stiffened in surprise, but didn't stop her as her lips crushed into his. He returned the kiss briefly before pulling away. "It is not time for—"

Moaning, Paige pressed forward again. She didn't care that they had a few hours left before the official ending of the intention courting time. She drank in the taste of his lips, wanting to devour him. It had been too long and his taste was too good. The warm contours of his firm body rubbed into her chest until her breasts ached for more contact.

Aidan groaned. His hands gripped her ass tight, lifting her from the floor to keep them together. He kissed her so hard his teeth cut into her mouth and she made a small noise of surprise. "Ow."

"My apolo—"

"I love you," she said, the words flowing out of her.

"You, ah..." He blinked in obvious surprise. Not letting go of her ass, he kept her pressed against him. However, the swaying of his body had stopped and she got the impression he gripped her more because he was taken by surprise by her declaration than anything else.

"I realize what you said, that Starian men do not put much stock in love, but I love you and I think you love me. Actually, I know it even if you do not." Paige caressed his cheek, brushing cool, wet hair from his face. The fingers digging into her ass cheeks flexed but didn't let go. She felt the unmistakable press of his cock to her stomach. "I can wait for you to say it because I know that someday you will know it too."

"What? How? Did Oracle Teena say such a thing? Because this does not sound like something a

Starian oracle would say. We are not trained to give credence to such sentiments."

"I hardly found Oracle Teena's predictions impressive. She will have to do more than mumble a few words and change her eye color to impress me." Paige arched a brow. "You forget, Sir Aidan, you are with an oracle right now. I know things."

"But, you see death from the weather. That is hardly the same as seeing what you claim."

"Yes, I do see death. But it would seem I also see life now. Perhaps you were right. This is the right place for me with my curse." Paige grinned. Her feet dangled and she wrapped her arms around his neck.

"And you saw that I love you?"

"Yes." She nodded, waiting for his stunned expression to fill in. Two fortnights ago his hesitance in this situation would have hurt her. Then, she wouldn't have thought him capable of loving her as she had come to love him. Now she understood him and his ways. He'd been raised a warrior, a soldier, a man of honor and duty. The notion of love was going to be new to someone like that. But her vision gave her hope, and his future words tore down the last of her hesitance and defenses. He might not be able to say the words today, or even understand them, but someday he would and that was good enough for Paige.

"And you saw me tell you this?"

"Yes." Nodding again, she added, "You were quite old with short, gray hair and very handsome lines in your face. And you said to me, 'You have always had my heart, my lady.' I heard it as clear as I hear you now. You love me."

"And this pleases you?" He finally began to move, adjusting her against him without setting her on the floor.

"It pleases me very much." Paige licked her lips. His body felt so good, so right.

"If you are pleased, my lady, then I am pleased." Aidan took her mouth, as if pouring into her all the unspent passions that had built up inside him.

"Oh wait," Paige pushed on him. "We cannot. Not yet."

Aidan groaned. "Please, by all the bloody battle axes in Staria, do not tell me we have to go another two fortnights. I cannot take denying myself of you."

Paige laughed, pushing at his chest so he let her go. Aidan groaned loudly before making small, pouting noises behind her. She found the knife on the floor and picked it up. "I need to cut you first."

Completely unconcerned, he said, "I have not played this game before."

"The exchanging of blood," Paige answered. "Roll up your sleeve."

Instead of listening, he pulled his tunic over his head and threw it onto the table. He loomed over her with stalking grace, lowering his chin and narrowing his eyes. Paige trembled. He came to her and lifted her knife hand. His fist wrapped hers, controlling the blade. He brought the tip to the center of his chest and traced the flat of the blade downward, not drawing blood.

"Where would you like to cut, my lady?" His words were low and seductive. When he reached his stomach, he lifted the blade to his lips and licked the pointed tip.

"I, ah..." Paige swallowed, fascinated by the movements of his tongue.

"Yea, Lady Paige?" he whispered.

"Arm," she answered, the word hardly audible.

Aidan let go of her hand and held out his arm.

"The other one."

His seductive grin widened and he offered his opposite arm. "Here. Cut. Take what you need of me. It all belongs to you anyway."

Her hand trembled nervously as she took the

blade and put it to his forearm. The sharp dagger moved over him, but didn't cut. Aidan laughed. "You will have to push harder than that, my lady. My skin is not as soft as yours."

Paige tried it again, making a light wound. He kept his eyes on her, not flinching, not showing any pain. When blood beaded on his flesh, she gave him the blade and turned her arm so the palm of her hand faced upward.

"Shouldn't you remove your tunic as well?" Aidan grinned hopefully. She gave a small laugh, but didn't move to undress.

"Please make it fast," Paige said, holding out her arm. She bit the inside of her lip and narrowed her eyes, waiting for the pain. Aidan drew the blade so fast it took her a moment to realize he'd finished. A small trail lined her arm and she turned it over, pressing her wound to his.

"I will never harm you again, Sir Aidan, this union is sealed. We are one," she whispered.

Aidan leaned into her. "I cannot hear you, my lady. You are too quiet."

Paige cleared her throat, repeating louder, "I will never harm you again, Sir Aidan, this union is sealed. We are one." Then she continued the traditional words, "Our blood now flows through each other and as I live for you, you now live for me."

"I will never harm you, sweet Lady Paige, this union is sealed. We are one." He brushed his lips along the corner of her mouth. "Our blood now flows through each other and as you live for me, I live for you." Aidan paused. "Is that how it is done? Are we finished? Or should I say you are claimed?"

Paige shook her head in denial. "Finished? Oh no, my husband. We are just getting started."

AIDAN WATCHED his wife's ass as she led him down the hall, past the chamber she'd been using. She paused by his bedchamber door, pushing it open to lead him inside. He found the way she'd hesitated to cut him adorable, though the wound she inflicted hardly hurt. It wouldn't even leave a scar. Already, it had stopped bleeding, as had hers. Aidan had found he didn't want to mar her pretty flesh, though if it was what she needed to know he was serious, that she was his, then he'd obey her wish.

Her words had shocked him with their certainty, *I realize what you said, that Starian men do not put much stock in love, but I love you and I think you love me. Actually, I know it even if you do not.*

Paige believed what she said. He saw it in her eyes when she said she loved him. The words, though startling, did something to him. They made him consider more—more beyond duty and responsibility.

His room looked much like the chambers at Battlewar, bigger than other rooms in the house, but sparse in décor. The large bed next to a cushioned dressing chair held his attention through the corner of his eyes. Before he could push her down onto it and fall on top of her, Paige pulled him into her and began kissing him. Her hands ran all over his body, touching everywhere she could reach as he tugged the laces of her corset bodice. With eager precision, he stripped her of her clothes before setting to work on his pants. Before his breeches fell to the ground, he had his lips on her breasts, sucking and licking the hard nipples.

Turning him, she pushed him down on a chair, forcing him to sit. He reached for her, but she slowly spun so her ass was to him. She backed up, lifting her arms behind her head while she rubbed her ass along his cock. Aidan grabbed her chest, squeezing as she moved along him. His cock ached with need. It had been too long since he felt the close heat of her body, the wet clamp of her pussy. Even their wanton encounter behind the stables didn't calm his ardor.

"Ah, Paige, methinks we should discuss—" Aidan tried to force her more fully onto his lap. He rocked his hips into her, molding it to the soft cleft of her ass.

"Shh," she hushed. "This is our wedding night. Let's just enjoy it."

She massaged his cock with her ass, circling her hips. He grabbed her breasts, holding her down against him to keep the pressure tight as he rubbed against the warm, dry flesh. Pushing up, she finally faced him, only she didn't climb on his lap as he wanted. Instead, she got to her knees and parted her lips. Paige flipped her hair over her shoulder, out of her way. He jerked before she even touched him with her wet mouth.

Paige sucked him between her lips, her whole body working erotically as she moved over him. He kept his hands at his sides, letting her have complete control. She reached up his chest, scratching him as she moved up and down, up and down, sucking and licking and biting. Every glide and pull caused his body to tense and shudder. He gripped the arms of the chair. He closed his eyes and bit his lip, trying to hold back, but her suctioning lips demanded he give her everything. Aidan came between her lips, mesmerized by the lapping way she enthusiastically drank him in.

She stopped, smiling at him as she licked his juices from her lips. "I like your taste."

He groaned, reaching for her, but she swatted his hand.

"I know you like watching me." She wiggled her body in front of him, leisurely swaying and spinning in a seductive dance. Her hand moved, forcing his eyes to follow them as she touched her thighs, her breasts, her glistening pussy. "I want you hard again."

It was a desire he would have no problem granting. Already he felt his shaft stirring. "I want *you* again."

* * *

Paige felt no inhibition in knowing Aidan watched her. She knew he cared for her, saw the desire in his eyes. The feeling was empowering, as was the knowledge she could control the warrior with just one look or touch.

Aidan shot up from his chair, grabbing her from behind. Strong, calloused hands slid over her tingling flesh, exploring where her hands had just roamed.

The growing evidence of his renewed desire brushed the back of her hip. Aidan swept her hair aside, kissing her throat, the nape of her neck, the long line of her spine. He traveled, kneeling behind her. Teeth nipped her ass cheek as hands roamed her thighs. She had yet to find her release and each sensation was amplified twentyfold.

Aidan slipped his finger along her wet slit, parting her sex. He probed her pussy, thrusting his finger inside her only to wiggle it around. He moaned against the side of her hip. Paige touched his head, massaging his scalp.

Aidan rose to his feet and his finger slid from inside her. Gently, he lifted her into his arms and laid her on the bed. Starting at her toes, he massaged his way up her legs until she worked her feet against the mattress.

"Aidan, please," she begged, trying to sit up so she could pull him up. "Please, I need you."

Aidan crawled over her, forcing her onto her back. He licked her breasts, devouring them as he sucked her nipples deep into his mouth. Her legs worked against him as she tried to force him up. Finally, he pushed her thighs open with his. Her hips searched for him.

Aidan touched her again with his hand and she

was certain he was trying to torture her. Steamy eyes watched her thrash about. He rubbed her, circling her swollen lips and clit with precision. She panted and cried out, sighing and moaning at the feel of him. When he felt her body begin to tremble, he pulled back.

"I need you," Paige whispered, reaching for him.

Aidan groaned, not hesitating as he brought his cock to her willing body. He was so handsome, his bronzed body so perfect. He thrust forward, filling her, taking away the ache of their fortnights of being apart. Nothing mattered, nothing existed beyond the look in his eyes, the feel of his tongue, the sound of his harsh breath.

Unyielding hardness mixed with scalding heat. He braced his weight with one hand while roaming her body with the other, moving it smoothly over her flesh. He kept his movements deep and small, exerting pressure in all the right places. Paige moaned, overcome with raw, unrefined emotions.

Paige caressed his neck and jaw before pulling his face down to hers for a kiss. Aidan quickened his pace as her tongue slid past his lips. She squirmed beneath him, her knees lifting to tighten along his waist.

"Aidan, ah," she tried to speak into his lips,

wanting to say all the things swimming around inside her. All that came out was a series of moans and pants. Logical thought and reason left her. Her heart hammered so loud she heard it thundering in her ears.

Aidan broke the kiss, lifting up for better leverage. He rocked against her core, moving faster and harder. Paige watched his muscles rippling in his chest, fascinated by the way the shadowed light appeared to dance over him.

Tension built low in her belly, the agonizing pleasure almost more than she could bear. Paige cried out, not caring who heard her. She held on tight to his biceps, digging her fingernails into the thick muscles as she quaked uncontrollably. Seconds later, Aidan's cry joined hers. He buried himself hard and so deep she was sure he touched her very soul.

Paige's moan turned into a soft pant before fading into an incoherent whimper. Her limbs fell weakly to the bed. Aidan rolled next to her and pulled her into his arms. Holding her tight, he said, "I would like for you to stay with me tonight."

"You'll sleep with me every night. I plan on staying forever." Paige sighed, smiling happily as she let the softness of sleep lull her into its depths.

EPILOGUE

"I DO NOT WISH to go to a fire ceremony at Battlewar," Paige protested, dragging her feet as Aidan tried to lead her to her horse. Behind her, Carrina laughed. She wasn't sure if the woman chuckled at the young couple fighting over a man's duty to attend the ceremony and Paige's abhorrence for any town bigger than Fallenrock Village, or the antics of Shana's boys as they stick-fought across the yard. The children visited often to train with Aidan. Paige found she didn't mind their company at all.

"I have already told you, my sweet lady, there is nothing you can say to make me sway my course. We were invited and, as honored guests who are new to marriage, we should attend. The king gave me leave from my duties to make an appearance."

"But, I must go to visit the other oracles. They told me I had to go back to them if I saw a vision." Paige put her hand dramatically to her forehead and moaned. "I'm seeing falling trees. The Hanging Forest is on fire. Animals stampeding. People screaming. Your horse—"

"A good effort," he laughed, "but I can tell when you have a real vision. And you have had several visions since visiting with the other oracles, Oracle Paige, and have not once gone back since your first visit."

"I would be there every day. I have no desire to tell them I can predict the daily weather. If they found out, they would probably try to give me a white robe and make me practice those moves Teena does." Paige held her arms to the side and began to mimic Oracle Teena's walk, the gliding self-importance combined with wide, overdramatic movements.

Aidan chuckled.

Paige let her lashes fall over her eyes as she tugged a suddenly pliable Aidan toward her. Licking her lips, she said in a breathy whisper, "Are you sure there is nothing I can do to convince you?"

"We may," Aidan cleared his throat, "do *that* when we get to Battlewar." He gave her a meaningful once-over. "Perhaps on the way as well, my lady."

Aidan kissed the tip of her nose, tugging her insistently behind him. "You have your new gown. Most ladies would be pleased to show it off."

"I'd be pleased to take it off," Paige said, glancing down at the green gown with the gold corset. It was a beautiful gown, one of several her husband bought for her. "Please let's not go."

"We must. Now, no more argument." He continued to walk toward the stables. "Besides, we have reason to celebrate."

"Oh?" she arched a brow. "And what reason is that?"

"I received a missive from the king this morn."

Her heart nearly stopped beating and this time no amount of pulling could make her move. "You have been ordered back to the battlefront, haven't you? I knew this day would come, that you would have to go, but so soon? How long? Can I go with you?"

"I'm ordered to a new battlefront," Aidan said. Then, frowning, he commanded, "And no, you cannot go to the battlefront."

"New?" Paige began to pace. "King Wilhelm is sending you over the borders, isn't he? I have had a feeling someone will be going over the borders. I never thought it would be—"

"Paige, calm yourself. I will not die in battle."

"Oh, I know." She nodded in agreement. "I already saw you as an old man. But that doesn't mean you cannot be hurt, or gone for years."

"I'm to guard something very precious." He held onto his wrist, putting his hand over the tattoo.

"Well, I hope it's a rock in the middle of the forest." She refused to smile, even as he gave her the most adorable look.

Aidan tilted his head to the side and began looking her over. "A rock? No, that is not how I would describe it."

Paige glanced behind her before chuckling. "Why don't you tell me?"

"The king ordered me to stay in Fallenrock. Caniba spies were found in the forest north of the border. They have been stopped, but it has been decided that the oracles need more protection. So, I'm in charge of the new encampment outside Fallenrock Castle. It is less than an hour's ride from here." He reached for her, pulling her into his arms.

"So, you're saying you will always be around? That I will never be rid of you?" she asked, trying to maintain a straight face.

"Unless you had other plans for your life, my lady." He kissed the tip of her nose.

"Well, Baker Fredrick from the village is in need of a wife and Merrit says a minimum of ten husbands are ideal to run a proper household." Paige barely got the words out before Aidan had her tight to his chest. He lifted her feet off the ground with a growl. She laughed, squealing as he spun her around in a circle. "I jest, I jest!"

He set her back down. "Good, because I will never approve of a second husband. You are mine. Only mine."

Paige wrapped her arms around his neck, letting her body fall into his. "Only yours, Aidan. I love you."

Then, to her surprise, he answered, "And you will always have my heart, my lady."

Unsure she'd heard him right, she asked, "Did you just say...?"

"I love you too, Paige. I see your face and my chest tightens. I think of you and my lips smile. I might not understand it, or why the gods would wish it to be so, I only know that you are the greatest reward a warrior could ever receive. I love you. I should have said it sooner, but..."

"But you are a warrior and warriors are not taught about love," she finished for him. "I understand, my love."

"Now, come. We really must ride." He swept her up into his arms, carrying her toward the stables. "There is nothing you can say to—"

"I'm with child," Paige announced. Behind her the boys began to giggle. Carrina screamed, happily clapping her hands.

Aidan finally stopped moving. His eyes widened in shock but he didn't set her back down. "You are certain?"

"The midwife is." Paige gave a small grin. Then, louder, she yelled over her shoulder, "It's either that or your mother has been cooking marriage potions into her food again."

"I have not!" Carrina protested. "Not since you two made your marriage right."

"I hope you kept the recipe." Paige winked at Aidan so Carrina couldn't see. "I have invited Martin over to dine tonight."

Aidan hurried to the stables, passing the main door as he carried her behind the building to the private alcove. Setting her down, he knelt before and put his ear to her stomach. "My son." Then, looking up at Paige, his face filled with happiness, he whispered, "My heart."

Paige ran her hand into his hair, stroking him

gently as he continued to listen to her stomach. Everything was perfect.

You will always have my heart, my lady.

The End

TAKING KARRE

THE SERIES CONTINUES...

Divinity Warriors Book Four
by Michelle M. Pillow

Alternate Reality Romance

Sir Vidar of Spearhead is too busy guarding the borderlands to bother with the headache of selecting a bride. Ordered to marry by the king, he plans to grab a woman and get back to the warfront, never to think of it again. That is until he meets the alluring Lady Karre with her teasing eyes, lush lips and irresistible ways.

Known by many names, inter-dimensional thief Karre, has only one purpose—take down the company that ruined her life. When her luck runs out and she's caught, Divinity Corporation condemns her to matrimony on a primitive, warrior-filled plane where Karre soon discovers there are worse fates than being prisoner to a man with insatiable appetites.

Before long, days and nights filled with bliss becomes something neither expected, and when Karre is taken, Vidar is forced to confront emotions a battle-hardened warrior never expected to feel.

Taking Karre Prologue Excerpt

Three weeks ago, Dimensional Plane 395, Adult Pleasure Centre VWH
Because right now, in this moment, she was their fantasy.

Karre marched out on stage in red stiletto heels, a slinky dress, big grin and nothing else. She kept tempo with the hard, drumming beat of music. Men hollered, whooping their excitement just to see her. She smiled at them, looking over the crowd of heads. She could make them do anything—beg, buy, steal, kill—because right now, in this moment, she was their fantasy.

Blonde hair piled high on her head, garnished

with a string of diamonds and rubies some suitor had given her. It was a sweet trinket, one she might even keep, not that she would remember where the jewels came from. She traveled too much and had more important things on her mind.

Karre turned slowly with her arms raised above her head. The hem of her short dress lifted to just below the curve of her ass. When her back was to the crowd, she bent forward. The cheering grew as the men got a peek of the naked treasure hidden beneath the clinging silver. What did she care if they saw her ass? Her pussy? Her breasts? They were just skin, flesh, a tool like any other. No matter how much they wanted her, they would never be able to touch her.

On this dimensional plane of existence, humans cohabitated with humanoid creatures. The first time Karre saw a vampire sucking on the neck of a shifted werewolf, she'd nearly sprinted out of the room to find her wrist portal to flash out of there to another plane. The portable device looked like a large bracelet to most, but to Karre it was her sole means of survival.

Necessity made her stay where she was. This plane was the easiest to get jewels on without resorting to thievery and the hard, shiny rocks were good for trade in nearly every dimension. Besides, not counting the dancing, being in Dimensional Plane 395 was like taking a vacation. With so many strange and different creatures, they never questioned anything she said and most were focused more on blood-drinking and pleasure-seeking.

Being in a new dimensional plane was like being in your world, but only if had it evolved in a different way. To a point, there were many similarities. Languages, generally, were relatively similar, though for some reason the written word consisted of unfamiliar symbols. Some people looked the same, but were not the same people. Natural disasters and major human events were shared. Weather was the same and each place was still Earth.

"I adore you, Sparkle!" a man yelled. "Marry me!"

Karre turned to look over her shoulder at the crowd and winked. A plethora of large green horns, red flesh, reptile skin, webbed fingers, sharp fangs, and ridged flesh stretched out before her until the mass became a single entity flowing back and forth like a wave.

"I'll take that as a yes," the same voice answered her playful flirting. A rush of similar proposals followed the first, showering her in declarations of love. But she wasn't fool enough to believe them. What they felt wasn't love. It was lust.

Karre knew their adoration for what it was and used it to fuel her dance. She twirled and wiggled, thrust her ass toward them, drew her hips in seductive circles, only to pause in a sexy pose in time with the music. Slowly, she undressed, peeling the slinky gown off her body. Several lights flashed, illuminating her from various angles, leaving no curve unseen.

Just flesh. Just a means. Just another job. Just another plane and soon a distant memory.

Her smile widened, as she knew this was her last dance, at least for this trip. The cheering rose, but she stopped listening. And then it was over. Karre held still, letting the dying notes find their silence before walking naked from the stage.

"You were wonderful tonight, Sparkle," a new dancer fawned. "The crowd loves you. I was wondering if you'd show me how to—"

"Is he here?" Karre asked, stopping the woman from starting a conversation Karre didn't have time for. It's not like she could tell the truth—that all her dancing skill was someone else's memories uploaded into her brain by a device she'd bartered for on another plane.

"He's in your room," the woman answered, frowning slightly at having her question dismissed. "And he brought a large case. I think it's full of gifts so you'll consider his suit."

"Perfect," Karre grinned. Taking a long robe the woman held out, she slipped it over her shoulders. "I don't want to be disturbed."

Two weeks ago, Dimensional Plane 1 5 4, Stac Lesh Mansion
Because right now, in this moment, she was the help.

Karre stared at her red, curly hair in the liquid-silver reflection wall. It had been pulled into a bun at the nape of her neck. The long skirt of the plain uniform and padded body suit did much to hide her figure under the thick gray wool. An apron, changed every time so much as a spot marred the pristine white, covered high over her chest and low to her knees. With the clothes and makeup to pale her face into an unimpressive mask, no one would look twice in her direction because right now, in this moment, she was the help.

She had expected to keep her head down and do her job for months before coming back into this room. But in putting on the uniform, she became invisible. The rich people she worked for didn't look in her direction twice. Well, that wasn't necessarily true. When the wife was gone, the husband had looked at her more than twice. A big grin showcasing blacked-out teeth and a very inappropriately timed belch had changed his interest quickly.

Karre reached to touch her reflection. Behind her, the rich baby's room spread out like the entrance to a palace. Gilded ceilings etched with clouds, golden rays of light and ridiculously cheerful fat angels stretched above as white marble stretched below. It was cold and unwelcoming and more than any one person deserved.

"Oh, wonderful, finally, help," the rich wife said, sweeping into the room. Karre didn't bother to learn the lady's name. "Rich wife" was much easier to remember. The woman held her child under the arms, away from her chest, as if contact with the baby would somehow ruin her carefully planned outfit. "Which one are you?"

"Brigitte, ma'am."

"Take Cinny," the woman ordered. "Mommy needs time to collect herself."

Karre suppressed her groan of frustration at being interrupted and stood to dutifully take the child. She cradled the poor creature close and walked it toward the crib.

"Sing to Cinny before you put her down," rich wife ordered, standing before the liquid silver as she brushed at her clothes.

Karre stopped walking. Sing? To the gurgling, wiggling mass in her arms?

"Well, Brigitte?"

"Mistress, mistress, let me come in," Karre sang the only childlike-sounding song she could think of at the moment, pausing to clear her throat. "I have the pence if you have a quim."

"What a pretty tune," the woman said. "I've never heard it. What does it mean?"

"My dad sang it to my mom," Karre answered, letting the memories she had uploaded into her mind take over her personality—Brigitte of the Fallen Women, a whore's daughter raised in a brothel, adept at blending into new environments. She left off the word "once" before adding the lie, "I'm not sure what it means."

"Carry on."

"Mistress, mistress, I'm stiff as a pin. I need your..." Karre continued, lowering her voice as the woman left her alone with the gurgling, oblivious child. Stopping, she laid the baby down and said, "Sorry, kid, it's the only song I knew the words to. But I guess it's all right. I turned out just fine with lots of jewels and pretty things and you're too little to understand what any of it means. You should be more worried about growing up in this place with that mom of yours. Now, if you just be good," she paused and tucked a blanket around the infant's body, "I've got a job to do."

Going back to the wall, Karre again reached for her reflection. She stepped forward, letting the liquid hit her hand. It stung, freezing cold in the warm room. For a moment, she hesitated, glancing back at the gurgling child. She thought about grabbing Cinny and taking the baby with her.

"Sorry, kid," she whispered, "even with that mother, you're better off here."

It was a delicate balance—keeping her purpose in her mind while living out the personality and quirks of another—almost like having two people in her head. Karre's hand met with the wall as she felt around, searching for the device she'd hidden. When her fingers met with a smooth, flat surface, she frowned. Putting a second hand to the wall she became frantic, sliding her palms in wide, searching arcs. Perhaps the adhesive she used had come loose. She bent her knees, crouching as she searched the bottom corner of the liquid reflecting wall. Her fingers were so cold it became hard to feel, but the molecular structure of the liquid kept the silver from trickling down her arms as it remained bonded to itself.

Then, to her great surprise, warmth gripped her. A hand wrapped her wrist and jerked her forward. She was pulled through the wall, feeling the sting of silver before landing on a hard, stone floor. Gasping and shivering, she looked around the secret room. A wall of computing towers lined one side, next to three technicians silently typing away on their holographic keypads.

"Lose something, Brigitte?" a man asked, coming close.

Karre glanced up from the floor, "No, sir. I have nothing to lose."

"You are extraordinary." The man laughed. Her eyes instantly took in the familiar insignia of the Divinity Corporation. "Finally, we meet."

Karre forced a grin she didn't feel, letting him see her blackened teeth. Knowing what she looked like, she couldn't help but wonder at his choice of words.

Extraordinary? "I wasn't aware we were destined to meet, sir. How lucky for me."

"I can assure you when I'm done with you, you won't feel lucky." The man leaned down, studying her face. He had the militant rigidity of a soldier, from the purposeful jerks of his body to the engraved frown lines around his mouth and eyes. His hard gaze bored into her, filling her with cold dread. She, or rather Brigitte, had seen that look in men's eyes before. They were usually the kind to beat a prostitute the second they couldn't get their pricks hard.

"I've heard that one before," she mumbled, pretending to be unimpressed.

"I'm Director Tomes and..." He paused, lifting the small, wrist-wrapping device she'd been searching the liquid-silver wall for. Divinity had the only known source of top-secret inter-dimensional travel technology and they wouldn't like the fact that someone had stolen it. "I have a feeling you know where I am from. It was very naughty of you to borrow our only portable jump prototype. Our scientists will be very interested in seeing how you got it to work. This device will make traveling to uncharted worlds much easier. No more carting around temporary portals. No more perfectly timed pickups from headquarters. No more rescue parties."

Less supervision so you can do more dark deeds, Karre silently added.

"We'll be able to explore planes at a much faster rate," Tomes continued, as if it was a good thing.

Just like an infectious disease.

"Sorry, I'm not available for science lessons, but if you'd like to make an appointment, I'm sure I can fit you in," Karre hummed in pretend thought, "uh, never."

"Oh, you're going to be fun to break, my dear," Tomes promised. "Talbert. Get her ready to go."

For a complete, up-to-date booklist, visit www. MichellePillow.com

ABOUT MICHELLE M. PILLOW

***New York Times* & *USA TODAY*
Bestselling Author**

Michelle loves to travel and try new things, whether it's a paranormal investigation of an old Vaudeville Theatre or climbing Mayan temples in Belize. She believes life is an adventure fueled by copious amounts of coffee.

Newly relocated to the American South, Michelle is involved in various film and documentary projects with her talented director husband. She is mom to a fantastic artist. And she's managed by a dog and cat who make sure she's meeting her deadlines.

For the most part she can be found wearing pajama pants and working in her office. There may or may not be dancing. It's all part of the creative process.

Come say hello! Michelle loves talking with readers on social media!

www.MichellePillow.com

facebook.com/AuthorMichellePillow

twitter.com/michellepillow

instagram.com/michellempillow

bookbub.com/authors/michelle-m-pillow

goodreads.com/Michelle_Pillow

amazon.com/author/michellepillow

youtube.com/michellepillow

pinterest.com/michellepillow

COMPLIMENTARY EXCERPTS

TRY BEFORE YOU BUY!

LILITH ENRAPTURED

BY MICHELLE M. PILLOW

Divinity Warriors Book One
Alternate Reality Romance

Sorin of Firewall lives in a land forever at war. In fact, the Starian men are so busy fighting, their marriage ceremony has been reduced to a "will of the gods" event where they simply pick a woman out of a lineup and claim her as a wife. With women becoming scarce, it's necessary to trade the offworld Divinity Corporation for brides. Duty-bound to attend the ceremony, he has no intention of picking a bride, let alone one from another dimension. That is, until he sees Lilith, the bewitching woman sent by the gods to reward—or punish?—him.

Lilith Enraptured Excerpt

Sorin took several deep breaths, feeling as he did when about to go into battle. Heat filled him as tension worked its way into his limbs. With a single thought, he could will his body to spring into action. He could erase her from the world and end this before it started.

But it was too late. He was lost the moment he'd looked at her, had seen her big blue eyes staring at him in trepidation. No, he was lost before that, when he felt her looking at him, beckoning him with her unwavering gaze to find her in the crowd.

Temptress. Witch.

He willed the desire inside him to go away. It shouldn't have been so strong. He'd relieved himself like he always did, had spilled his seed to ease the lonely ache.

Light from the fireplace shone through the white of her gown, silhouetting the long length of her legs and arms. The linen clung to her shoulders, swooping gently along the curves of her breasts— breasts that would be bare beneath. The tied hands were a new addition to the ceremony, thanks to Sir Aidan's wayward woman, Lady Paige. Sorin's barbaric side found he liked the addition.

Hunger rushed into every limb, lifting his cock beneath the long tunic. He didn't think to hide the reaction. No one would care. It had been so long, so very long, since he'd had a woman in his bed. He suppressed a groan. Soft flesh. Round breasts. Taut nipples. Slick, warm vessel to catch his passion. That certain female smell when he pressed his nose to her sex.

A thought whispered in the back of his mind. Maybe she's different. Maybe she'll be better. Maybe this one will stay.

He cursed the thought. No. She wasn't different. She wasn't better. Sorin had made up his mind long ago. He'd come, he'd look, but he never, ever wanted to find someone. He wasn't meant to have this, or her, or any kind of peace. Sorin was born into a land of war. He was made for it, every piece of him. One of the bloodiest battles in their history happened the very hour his mother gave birth to him.

Some were lucky to find peace in marriage, but not him. Tradition and necessity dictated he come to these ceremonies and try to find someone. He came from a noble line, a position of power, one that demanded he have sons to carry on his family's name. But society could not make him choose. It could not make him step forward and lay claim.

"Mine."

Where did that word come from? It sounded like his voice, booming over the hall to quiet all who watched into stunned silence. It felt like his body refusing to go to his place at the table, instead moving forward with arm uplifted to point at the blonde-haired beauty. But it couldn't be his body or his voice. That would mean he'd just announced his claim. Everyone would have heard it. He couldn't back out once the word was said.

"Sorin?" his younger brother, Ronen, hissed. Like Sorin, Ronen led one of the more renowned armies in all of Staria. Very few would dare to challenge their word or honor and the fact made it even more impossible for Sorin to take back what he'd done.

"Mine," Sorin found himself repeating. Was he possessed? What madness was this? He kept walking toward her. She merely stared at him, those wide, gorgeous eyes capturing his. Straight blonde hair hung long down her back, just as a woman's should.

"Brother?" Ronen questioned. The shock was evident in his voice. Sorin couldn't blame him for the surprise because that very day he'd been instructing Ronen to stay strong and not fall for a woman's pretty face. And what did Sorin do? He claimed a woman with a pretty face.

The hall remained quiet. Sorin stopped before the woman, noting with pleasure that she didn't cringe and fall away from his looming presence. Her strength would serve her well. Years of frustrated desires surged inside him. He couldn't put them off any longer. Deny it as he might, he needed a woman. He would never admit the words out loud. The need was not just for physical release, but for the softness of her, the sweet smell and the temporary relief from the endless fighting that such a creature could bring.

You tried this before, Sorin. Such things are not for you.

Fool.

Idiot.

Weak.

His accusing thoughts infuriated. Reaching for her bound arms, he took hold of the ropes. Not even his condescending inner voice could stop his actions. Sorin held her gaze steady, stating so she couldn't mistake his claim, "You are mine."

For a complete, up-to-date booklist, visit www.
MichellePillow.com

FIGHTING LADY JAYNE

BY MICHELLE M. PILLOW

Divinity Warriors Book Two
Alternate Reality Romance

Jayne Hart has earned her independence by becoming Divinity Corporation's inter-dimensional boxing champion. Life is great, until a dirty fighter knocks her unconscious. Now, abandoned by the corporation in a parallel world, Jayne will use every weapon she has to be free once more. Even if it means running from her sexy new "husband" and spending the rest of her life in a primitive forest.

Ronen of Firewall longs for a woman to warm his bed and his home, but he had no intention of choosing a bride. In an unprecedented move, one chooses him. Never in the history of the marriage ceremony has a woman dared to lay claim. How can he resist the alluring Lady Jayne? She's confident and sure in her decision to be with him—until their wedding night when she's nowhere to be found. But, Ronen is not one to shy from a battle. He will find Jayne and, when he does, he has one particular "weapon" in mind for taming his seductive, wayward wife.

Extended Prologue Excerpt

Getting her teeth knocked around in her head hurt like hell, but being able to spit blood into the face of her opponent more than made up for the discomfort. Jayne "The Sweet" Hart laughed as Big Bobby Bishop sputtered in anger. She knew he expected her to cry at the landed blow. Truth was, part of Jayne did want to cry. She wasn't a glutton for a beating, and that last hit had left blood running out of her mouth at a steady flow. They'd been going at it for nearly a half hour, bare-knuckle boxing—no protective gear beyond any sanctioned bioengineering, no referees, not like some of the other dimensions had. No, here on dimensional plane 241 almost anything was legal. That's why the gladiator ring paid such big money and drew the notice of rich, inter-dimensional travelers who could afford a private plane jump through Divinity Corporation. It's also why Jayne agreed to travel from her own world to this alternate reality where laws were more of a suggestion and killing someone in a fight was considered a good thing.

In many ways, each alternate reality was like drifting through time on her own home plane, had a singular event on the timeline been changed. Each dimension seemed to be a different outcome to a similar historical start. Some were so technologically advanced everything was done for them, and they'd found a worldwide peace and understanding. Jayne generally stayed away from those levels of existence. There wasn't much employment for fighters in such realities.

Other planes hadn't even developed a means of fast communication beyond throwing a bird into the air with a tiny letter tied to its leg. Still others had just installed their first aqueducts or invented their first vehicles to run without horses or oxen. Or, like 241, they had every technological comfort and yet somehow managed to maintain their barbarian sensibilities.

Any way you looked at it, Earth was Earth, just

different versions of itself—same languages, matching natural events, some people looked the same but weren't. Humans, for the most part, still resembled humans. And those with power were still greedy bastards trying to tell her how to do her job.

Big Bobby watched her expectantly, his mouth opened as if to scream in victory at any second. Jayne knew he expected her to fall with that punch. She watched as the excitement slowly died from his eyes, replaced by shock, then confusion, until finally a boiling rage. His eyes scanned the crowd before moving toward the large balcony to where his daddy sat watching. Big Bobby's father and known gangster boss had undoubtedly assured his halfwit-of-a-lug-nut son that he was a sure winner. It wouldn't have been so bad if Big Bobby had been an admirable opponent, but after a half hour, she could still see out of one of her eyes, and he only managed to knock her off her feet twice.

And Bossman Bishop wanted her to take a dive to this chump?

Jayne snorted. Not bloody likely. She'd never work as a boxer again—not that she had to. In her home dimension, she had plenty of money to bide her twelve lifetimes.

Divinity Corp paid her big for this fight. They

were her ticket home and had the only known source of inter-dimensional travel technology on this plane. Natural slips were extremely rare and the timing of them completely predictable by the company, even if they didn't know where the slip would go. If they didn't take her home, she'd be stuck until the end of time. Besides, there was no way she was taking a dive just because the local gangsters had promised to...

What had Bossman said again? Oh, yeah. They were going to gang rape her grandma while she watched. It had hardly been a threat. Jayne was an orphan. Still, a part of her was up in arms for the hypothetical grandmother they'd threatened.

There was no way Bossman could know about her lack of family. The publicity put out by Divinity Corp's entertainment division fostered the wholesome image of their Sweetheart Jayne. Of course, it was all a lie. They hired a family to take pictures with her at a rented country home—the devoted mother, the fake twin sister with a poor health condition, the baby brother and suit 'n' cravat dad.

The loud, almost fanatical cheering of the crowd grew. They surrounded on all sides, lining the rows upon rows of rotating theater seats. Every few minutes, the seats would shift, changing the angle from which a person watched. Lights flashed all around her. Floating cameras zipped by her head, but she ignored them. Most of the bets were on her and she never lost a fight. Never. And she would be damned if she gave this guy the reputation of being the one person who could take her down. He didn't deserve the title or her respect. Rage grew within her that he even dared to presume he was worthy of taking her down.

Do it for your family, Jayne, she thought sardonically.

Jayne decided to teach him and Bossman a lesson. She drew her body around, preparing to kick him upside the head in a move she knew he wouldn't see coming. Big Bobby swung again. She dodged the blow, and this time his hand merely grazed her cheek, stinging the cut she had there. She didn't hesitate. Whipping her leg around, she swung it for his head. Suddenly, every nerve in her body exploded with pain. There was no stopping her body's momentum as it lifted off the hard mat. The noise of the crowd faded and grew until stopping altogether. Big Bobby caught her suddenly slowed foot and pushed her backward. Nothing was as it should be. Lights streaked in her vision before her body was abruptly stopped by a metal pole slamming into her back.

Then, darkness clouded her mind and she could only think one thing.

Boxers' Poison.

For a complete, up-to-date booklist, visit www.MichellePillow.com

THE SAVAGE KING

BY MICHELLE M. PILLOW

Lords of the Var® Book One by Michelle M. Pillow
Bestselling Catshifter Romance Series

Cat-shifting King Kirill knows he must do his duty by his people. When his father unexpectedly dies, it's his destiny to take the throne and all of the responsibility that entails. What he hadn't prepared for is the troublesome prisoner that's now his to deal with.

Undercover Agent Ulyssa is no man's captive. Trapped in a primitive forest awaiting pickup, she's going to make the best out of a bad situation...which doesn't include falling for the seductions of a king.

About *Lords of the Var*® (Books 1-5)

You met their father, King Attor, in Dragon Lords Books 1-4, now meet the Var Princes!

The cat-shifter princes were raised to not believe in love, especially love for one woman, and they will do everything in their power to live up to their father's expectations. Oh, how the mighty will fall.

The Savage King Excerpt

Kirill watched the door to his bedroom open. He'd been sitting in the dark, trying to relieve the stress headache that had built behind his eyes for the last week. The pain started at the base of his skull and radiated up to his temples until he could hardly see straight.

A heavy responsibility had been thrust on his shoulders, a responsibility he really hadn't prepared himself for, the welfare of the Var people. King Attor had not left him in a good position. He'd rallied the people to the brink of war, convinced them that the Draig were their enemy, and even went so far as to attack the Draig royal family.

Kirill wanted to see peace in the land. However, he knew the facts didn't bode well for it. The Draig had a long list of grievances against King Attor and the Var kingdom.

Before his death, the king had ordered an attack on the four Draig princes, all of which ended horribly for the Var. The worst was when Prince Yusef was stabbed in the back, a most cowardly embarrassment for the Var guard who did it. If he hadn't been executed in the Draig prisons, he would've been ostracized from the Var community. Luckily, Prince Yusef survived or they'd already be at battle.

Attor had also arranged for the kidnapping of Yusef's new bride. The Draig Princess Olena had been rescued, or that too would've led to war. The old king had even tried to poison Princess Morrigan, the future Draig queen, on two separate occasions. She too lived. And those were only a few of the offenses Kirill knew about in the few weeks before King Attor's death. He could just imagine what he didn't know.

Kirill sighed, feeling very tired. He'd known since birth that the day would come when he'd be expected to step up and lead the Var as their new king. He just hadn't expected it to be for another hundred or so years. His father had been a hard man, whom he'd foolishly believed was invincible.

"Here kitty, kitty, kitty." His lovely houseguest's whisper drew his complete attention from his heavy thoughts.

Ulyssa bent over like she expected him to answer to the insulting call. He dropped his fingers from his temple into his lap, and a quizzical smile came to his lips. As he watched her, he wasn't sure if he was angered or amused by her words.

"Are you in here, you little furball?" she said, a little louder.

She wore his clothes. Never had the outfit looked sexier. His jaw tightened in masculine interest, as he unabashedly looked her over. All too well did he remember the softness of her body against his and the gentle, offering pleasure of her sweet lips. She'd made soft whimpering noises when he'd touched her, yielding, purring sounds in the back of her throat. Even with the aid of nef, he was surprised by how easily and confidently she melted into him. The Var were wild, passionate people and were drawn to the same qualities in others. He suspected she'd be an untamed lover.

Too bad she'd belonged to his father first. In his mind, that made her completely untouchable though none would dare question his claim if he were to take her to his bed. Technically, by Var law, she belonged to him until he chose to release her. For an insane moment, he thought about keeping her as a lover. He knew he wouldn't, but the thought was entertaining.

Kirill's grin deepened. Ulyssa strode across his home to the bathroom door with an irritated scowl. It was obvious she didn't see him in the darkened corner, watching her. He detected her engaging smell from across the room, the smell of a woman's desire. It stirred his blood, making his limbs heavy with arousal. And, for the first time since his father's death, his headache relieved itself.

"Hum, maybe I'm looking too high. I'm sure there has to be a little cat door here somewhere. Come here, little kitty. Where are you hiding?"

His slight smile fell at her words. It was easy to detect her mocking tone.

"Where's your little kitty door, huh?" Ulyssa whispered to herself, her blue gaze searching around in the dark.

Kirill grimaced in further displeasure. He watched her open the door to his weapons cabinet. Her eyes rounded, and he thought she might take one. She didn't. Instead, she nodded in appreciation before closing the door and continuing her search for an exit.

She stopped at a narrow window by his kitchen doorway. Her neck craned to the side, as she tried to see out over the distance. Kirill knew she looked at the forest. From under her breath, he heard her vehement whisper, "Where exactly did you little fur balls bring me? Ugh, I need to get out of this flea trap, even if I have to fight every one of you cowardly felines to do it. I've fought species twice as big and three times as frightening. A couple of little kitty cats don't scare me."

If this insolent woman wanted to play tough, oh, he'd play. Curling gracefully forward, Kirill shifted before his hands even touched the ground. He let one thick paw land silently on the floor, followed by a second. Short black fur rippled over his tanned flesh, blending him into the shadows. His clothes fell from his body, and he lowered his head as he crept forward. A low sound of warning started in the back of his throat. He was livid.

**To find out more about Michelle's books
visit www.MichellePillow.com**

PLEASE LEAVE A REVIEW

THANK YOU FOR READING!

Please take a moment to share your thoughts by reviewing this book.

Be sure to check out Michelle's other titles at www.michellepillow.com